"I really want to kiss you." Cash's hoarse voice ruffled her skin like sandpaper.

The desire stoked by the long ride pressed up against him and the vulnerability he'd expressed earlier flared, dazzling her. Penta licked her lower lip, accidentally brushing his thumb. His pupils, already dilated in the dim light, expanded further and he growled.

He growled.

Penta Unleashed, she reminded herself. She licked her lip again, this time deliberately swiping her tongue against his finger. "Why don't you, then?"

Cash's stormy gaze welded itself to Penta's, his light clasp on her chin tightening. She held herself still, waiting like a mouse in a trap. A willing mouse in a pain-free trap but caught all the same.

"I didn't think that was part of our agreement." The words ground out from between his tightly pressed lips.

"We didn't say it wasn't, either. We never discussed"—she swallowed and then made herself continue—"t-touching. And k-kissing." Damn it. She hadn't meant to stutter. But locked in the intensity of his expression, she was surprised she could form complete sentences at all.

"What we have isn't real. Touching you like this"— his fingers left her chin to trace the column of her throat in a fiery line—"shouldn't be allowed."

She knew it wasn't real. Could never be real. Being caressed by the tattooed hand of a hard but handsome man after breaking all sorts of speed limits on a motorbike and sneaking into a youth camp wasn't real, not in Penta's world. But she couldn't squash the wish that it was. That adventures with this man could be her reality.

Too Good for Words
(Silverberry Seduction Seasoned Romance Series,
Book Five)

By Brenda Margriet

COPYRIGHT PAGE

TOO GOOD FOR WORDS
(Silverberry Seduction Seasoned Romance Series, Book Five)

First edition published October 2023
Copyright © 2023 Brenda Margriet Clotildes
Digital ISBN 978-1-990697-05-0
Print ISBN 978-1-990697-04-3

Cover Art by K. B. Barrett Designs

To my co-hosts—Mellanie Szereto, Lily Baines, and Stephanie Morris—and the members of the Worth the Wait Seasoned Romance Readers Facebook Group—thanks for your support and encouragement, as well as your passion for romances celebrating older characters.

***

AUTHOR'S NOTE

In this story, the members of the Silverberry Book Club take a class that introduces them to riding a motorcycle. My expert beta readers kindly pointed out there is no such thing in most provinces and states. I did make a few minor changes to acknowledge this reality but would like to apologize for any inaccuracies that remain. Those mistakes are entirely mine.

Chapter One

Penta Potter woke with a start, her pulse accelerating to Indy 500 speed in a millisecond.

The front door closed with a quiet yet unmistakable thunk. The click of it opening must have been what had disturbed her moments before.

As the mother of a preteen, two teenagers, and a just-turned-twenty-one-year-old, her ears were finely honed to noises in the night. But all her children should have been safe in their beds.

A glance at her bedside clock showed 1:12 in glowing red numerals. Muffled voices filtered through her closed bedroom door. Both male, both irritated. One a gruff rumbling bass, the other a light reedy tenor.

Sliding out of bed, she retrieved the baseball bat she'd placed underneath it the first night she'd slept alone in the master suite she and Mark had shared. She'd had no occasion to use it, but knowing it was there reassured her.

Her right hand choking the smooth wood about one-third of the way up—the better for getting power behind the stroke—she eased open the door with her left and put her ear to the crack.

"Come on, dude." Her second son's sullen voice drifted up the stairs leading from the main floor to the bedroom level. "I'll tell her in the morning. I promise."

A fraction of the tension banding her shoulders relaxed, even as a new question arose. What was Cyril doing awake? He'd arrived home on the dot of eleven p.m., his Friday curfew, and grunted goodnight before disappearing to his room in the basement. She'd finished the movie she'd been pretending to watch as she waited and trailed up to her own room a few minutes later, ready to rest now all her chicks were at roost.

"How stupid do you think I am?"

The second voice had the hairs on the back of Penta's neck shivering to attention. So deep she could feel it in her toes. So menacing that if she'd had a tail, it would have tucked between her legs.

Her protective instincts roared, and she flew down the stairs, bare feet silent on the carpet, baseball bat raised above her head. "Who the hell are you and what are you doing with my son?"

Cyril's thin, gawky frame was eclipsed by the hulk of the man looming next to him. A black ball cap shadowed the stranger's eyes, and the lower part of his face was hidden by a full, dark red beard flecked with silver. Wide shoulders cloaked in black leather, and thick legs encased in soiled, tattered jeans completed the terrifying picture.

Penta's heart rate tripled, and she blinked dizziness away. Waggling the bat threateningly, she spoke through clenched teeth. "Well, who are you? Cyril, get over here." She jerked her head and stepped to the side, making room behind her.

"Jeez, Mom." Cyril hunched his shoulders, his expression an agony of humiliation. "What are you doing?"

"What do you think? I won't let him hurt you."

If anything, her pronouncement only increased Cyril's embarrassment. He muttered an obscenity. She'd deal with that offense later, after she'd taken care of the more pressing danger.

The stranger listened to this exchange with no softening of his flinty expression. "For fuck's sake, boy. Show your mother some respect." Since he used the same expletive, his command lost much of its force.

His words did, however, lessen her anxiety. A thug intent on mayhem surely wouldn't be worried about Cyril's filial obedience. "Will someone please explain what's going on?"

Cyril's posture lost all its belligerence as he shrank into himself like a turtle in a shell.

"Tell her." Big, Red, and Scary's tone brooked no rebellion.

Despite her growing conviction Cyril had done something dreadful, she was indignant. "Don't tell him what to do."

Big, Red, and Scary ignored her. "Spit it out."

His gaze drilled into Cyril's profile and her son ducked his chin even lower, wriggling his hips. Her heart sank. He'd done that since he was a toddler when caught sinning.

"Cyril? What happened?" She realized she was still holding the baseball bat at shoulder height and let her arm drop to her side.

He muttered a few words, most of which were unintelligible.

Big, Red, and Scary took one step toward Cyril, who looked younger and frailer than ever. "Speak up."

"Me and the guys broke some windows. At his shop." He jerked his head in a minuscule movement toward the stranger.

"And?" The single syllable uttered in a quiet growl was more terrifying than any shout.

Cyril drew in a long shaky breath and revealed the rest in one hurried rush, as if saying it fast would make it sound less horrible. "And we knocked over a couple motorbikes and messed up some displays and tried to break into a drawer where we thought there might be money. And the other guys got away, but he caught me." Another tiny twitch toward his accuser.

Penta wanted to sink to the floor and weep for the loss of innocence—both hers and Cyril's. But she didn't have time to fall apart. She had to get Big, Red, and Scary out of the house before her other children appeared, wondering what was going on.

"I'm sure he's very sorry for doing such a terrible thing." She glared at Cyril, which was less than effective since his gaze was glued to the floor. "You can be sure he'll be suitably punished."

"I know he will. Because he's going to clean up the mess. And work for me until the value of the damage is paid off."

Cyril's head jerked up. "Am not."

Big, Red, and Scary ignored him. Fishing in a pocket inside his coat, he pulled out a business card and handed it to Penta.

She took it automatically, noting the grime edging his fingernails, the dark lines of a tattoo covering the back of his hand. She shuddered. No way was Cyril spending any amount of time with this man, no matter what crimes he had committed. "I'm his mother. I'll decide what punishment he deserves. As for the damages, I'll pay them."

He ignored her declaration as he had Cyril's protest. "Eight o'clock at the shop. He knows where it is." His tone was bleakly amused. "If he doesn't come, I'm calling the cops and pressing charges."

He opened the door, stepped into the night, and closed it behind him with quiet finality.

Cash Rylance climbed into his pickup and stared at the house.

The conventional 1980s four-level split with double garage was painted a boring beige and tan. Streetlights illuminated a shaggy lawn with a large round garden in the middle, both starting to green now it was past the May long weekend and the weather was warming up. Inside, he'd seen school photos on the wall, a clutter of shoes on the floor, and a sport bag tossed casually by the door.

All evidence of middle-class comfort and a normal, pleasant family life.

He thumped his fist violently on the steering wheel. "Goddamn idiot." The kid—Cyril—appeared to come from the kind of home Cash had dreamed of when he was the same age. But did he appreciate it? Not likely, given the mischief he and his buddies had been up to.

Of course, things weren't always as they seemed. Maybe he was wrong about the heart-broken love he'd seen in the woman's eyes when she'd realized her son was a vandal. Maybe the kid was acting out because of abuse or neglect. He wouldn't lay money on that, though. More likely, he was just a jerk who didn't know how good he had it.

Cash put the truck in reverse, rolled onto the empty road, and started back to his shop.

The image of Cyril's mother dashing down the stairs in her pink plaid pajamas while brandishing a baseball bat played before his eyes. Her curly brown hair had been pressed flat to one side of her head and a pillow crease marked her cheek. Abundantly rounded at hips and thighs, her unbound breasts jiggling invitingly under the light fabric, her eyes had sparked with fierce lightning despite the fear he'd heard trembling in her voice.

She was a warrior, intent on protecting her young. And even though he'd been furious at her son and still reeling from the damage inflicted on his beloved shop, he couldn't repress a stir of interest.

Not that anything could come of it. He was the last person a respectable, loving, suburban mom would look at twice. Besides, there was probably a husband somewhere, even though he hadn't shown his face tonight.

He arrived at his shop via the back alley and parked in one of the three narrow slots. A metal staircase led up to his apartment, where peaceful solitude would greet him. Instead, he went through the door that led to the main floor.

The teens' rampage hadn't made it to the rear of

the building, so the large room where he kept spare parts and other supplies was untouched. Who knew what havoc they would have wreaked if he didn't live on site. He had an alarm system—it had alerted him *after* the sound of smashing glass had jolted him awake—but it was mainly because his insurance policy demanded it and wasn't connected to local police or a security service. Why bother when he rarely went anywhere else and had no qualms about protecting his possessions with any actions necessary?

At the end of a short hall, he stepped into the space taking up three-quarters of the main level and his fury rose again. Light from the street glittered on thousands of shards of scattered glass. In the partially intact windows on either side of the decimated front door, star-shaped fractures sparkled like supernovas. The Honda Gold Wing and Harley Softail he'd just finished babying into smooth-running perfection sprawled on the concrete floor, surrounded by the helmets, gloves, and other accessories that had been swept off the steel display shelves.

Pain blossomed in his palms and knuckles. He'd clenched his fists so tightly his hands were cramping. Hot, terrible anger rose like a red tide from his gut to the back of his throat, demanding release. Closing his eyes, he breathed deeply through his nose, held it until his chest ached, and then let the air trickle out of his mouth. He repeated this several more times before he trusted himself enough to open his eyes.

He snaked his way to the corner of the shop that was the heart of his business. The 1967 Triumph Tiger Cub he had just started restoring still stood propped on its kickstand and his lovingly cared for tools were undisturbed. As he had drowned in his first haze of fury, the fact the kids hadn't touched this area was all that had kept him from pummelling Cyril. The other four ruffians had managed to escape, but the kid had stumbled on a helmet and that tiny delay had been enough to allow Cash to grab the back of his skinny, acned neck in one hand and the ass of his baggy jeans in the other.

The boy's terrified shrieks had broken through his wild rage. Repressing his first inclination—tossing him through one of the damaged windows—he'd reined in his temper, dragged the boy to his truck, and given him a choice—police or home. White showing around his irises, Cyril had stuttered out his address. Though he'd regained some of his bravado on the short drive, Cash could sense the panic racing under his resentful posture. The boy's mother hadn't looked like anyone to be frightened of, despite her weapon, and Cyril hadn't cowered any more than expected by a teenager caught in the wrong. Still, Cash knew outwardly pleasant appearances could hide terrible secrets.

His threat to call the cops had been bullshit, anyway. He would never hand over a kid to be interrogated and manhandled by those bastards. He only wished he'd had someone to protect him from the same when he'd been that age.

No. Cleaning up the mess and doing grunt work for a few weeks would be punishment enough. Cash would make sure of it.

Chapter Two

Penta didn't bother setting an alarm when she crawled into bed for the second time that night. She wouldn't be able to sleep, not after her low-voiced yet contentious confrontation with Cyril.

She knew her divorce had affected her children. How could it not? Felix, the eldest, had become obsessed with getting good grades and insisted on working a part-time job, which she worried were his unnecessary efforts to replace his father as the head of the household. Delilah spent most of her time with her soccer teammates and only spoke to Penta when necessary, but since she was now fifteen this could be considered normal behaviour. Abra had been extra clingy for a long time, but had eventually reverted to her cheerful, petted, and pampered youngest child role.

Cyril had had the most dramatic and disturbing reaction. His school marks had slipped, and he'd stopped hanging out with his usual group of friends, taking up with a new gang. Penta had been uneasy about these unfamiliar boys from the start, despite no firm evidence.

Still, she knew who Cyril's co-conspirators were, though he refused to name them. It wasn't fair her son would be the only one punished simply because he'd been unfortunate enough to get caught. She'd pushed him as hard as she dared, but he'd remained tight-lipped, no matter how much she badgered. In the end she'd given up, sent him to bed, and staggered to her own room to spend the last hours of the night staring at the ceiling and wondering what she could have done differently.

Not just tonight. In so many aspects of her life.

At seven she heard the soft sounds of Felix moving about the kitchen. Normally she would have joined him for coffee before he headed to his weekend shift at Costco, but she didn't have the energy to pretend everything was fine. The mask she'd been wearing for years was getting harder and harder to don.

Several minutes later, the garage door rumbled up, Felix's car chugged out, and the door creaked down. He'd bought a battered, held-together-with-duct tape Honda Civic a year ago. She'd offered to help him buy something better, but he'd refused. His rejection had hurt. She was his mother. She should be allowed to make life easier for her children, not be condemned for it.

Speaking of condemned...

She rolled out of bed and made the trek to the basement where her two oldest children had tiny but separate spaces. The girls' bedrooms were across the hall from her own. She didn't expect them to make an appearance for a couple of hours. Time enough to get Cyril to Absolute Motorcycle Repair. It was only a few blocks away according to the card Big, Red, and Scary had given her.

Opening the door without knocking, she flicked on the light switch. "Time to get up, Cyril. I'll boil eggs for you before we go."

He screeched and scrambled to hide his bare, narrow chest with the sheet. "Mom! You're not allowed in my room!"

"I'm not in your room." She pointed at her toes, which hadn't crossed the threshold. "And you lost your right to privacy last night. Now get up. You have work to do."

He flopped back onto the mattress and covered his eyes with one scrawny arm. "I can't go back there. That dude was so angry."

She'd wrestled with this all night. On the one hand, the idea of Cyril spending time alone with the hard, grim man who'd dragged him home made her gut ache. On the other, he *had* vandalized the man's business. He deserved punishment.

"You're going. Now get out of bed." As reluctant as she was to deliver him, she had to see the damage for herself. Maybe it wasn't as bad as it sounded.

It was worse.

Penta stood just inside the door and stared, aghast. Most of the front of the shop was covered in plywood, since the windows were either non-existent or so badly cracked a toddler could have finished the job. Two gleaming monster motorbikes lay toppled, and an avalanche of items cascaded across the floor, everything dusted with chips of glass.

"Cyril!" At her side, he hunched his shoulders and wriggled his hips. "*You* did this?"

Big, Red, and Scary answered. "Him and four others at least. Needed that many to cause this much damage in so short a time. I live upstairs and came down as soon as I heard them."

"I don't know what to say." She waved her hand helplessly. "He's never done anything like this before. I'm so sorry."

"Not looking for apologies. Not from you." He turned his steel grey gaze on Cyril and pointed. "Go through that door there. You'll find flattened cardboard boxes. Set up two of them and bring them back here."

Penta swallowed down a demand he stop ordering her son around. Now she'd seen the full extent of the disaster, she could admit he had a right to be furious.

The cleanup would take at least a day, even with all three of them, so it was good she'd never intended to leave Cyril alone with the intimidating owner. Squaring her shoulders, she lifted her chin and did her best to meet the man's stony eyes. "I'll help too, Mr.—" Her mind blanked. She'd seen his name on the business card but for the life of her couldn't recall it now.

"Cash."

"Right. Where is your broom, Mr. Cash? I can start sweeping."

"Cash is my first name." Dark amusement glimmered in his gruff tones, though any hint of a smile was hidden by his full beard. "Why do you think you should help?"

She blinked, figuring the answer was obvious. He said nothing, waiting. She lifted her hands, palms up. "Cyril's my son. I'm responsible for him."

"He's how old?"

Her heart stuttered. Why did he want to know? Was he reconsidering his decision not to press charges? "Sixteen." Her mouth dried with fear.

"Old enough to own his actions." His tone was gentle but implacable. "Go home...Cyril's mom."

She scrambled for arguments that might change his mind as she absently answered the question indicated by his pause. "Penta. Penta Potter." An explosive snort drew her attention back to his face.

His amusement was obvious now, crinkling the corners of his eyes. "Really?"

"I know, it's ridiculous. I could have gone back to my maiden name after my divorce. It's Wicken, which is much better. But the kids were going to keep their father's, and I thought it would be too confusing." She was babbling, but his reaction had rattled her, set moths fluttering in her belly. His slight smile had made him seem...approachable. Friendly. Attractive.

None of which were thoughts she wanted to have.

She turned the conversation back to the matter at hand. "There's too much for Cyril to do by himself."

Cash raised his eyebrows. "You think I'd trust him on his own? I'll be here the whole time."

If he'd meant to reassure her, he failed. His words

only hardened her resolve. "I should stay."

Her son appeared from the back, sidling through the door with two large cardboard boxes tucked under his arms. He shot her a sullen look. "Go home, Mom. I don't want you here."

She stiffened, absorbing the pain of rejection. "I can help."

"I said I don't want you here."

His tone lashed her soul. She told herself it was just normal teenage rebellion, that he didn't mean to be rude. It still hurt.

Three quick steps put Cash in front of Cyril. His hands hung loose at his sides, his wide shoulders and strong back blocking her view. His navy-blue T-shirt had short sleeves and the tattoos she'd caught a glimpse of last night twisted and wound around his muscled forearms.

She couldn't hear his whispered words, only a deep bass growl. When he stepped aside, Cyril's gaze tracked him, wide-eyed and wary, before he looked at her. "I'm sorry, Mom. Thanks for offering. But I did this. I will clean it up."

Resentment bubbled. It wasn't Cash's place to reprimand her son. *She* was Cyril's parent, not him.

Before she could remonstrate against his highhandedness, he strode past and opened the door. Brilliant sunlight flared into the room made dim by the plywood on the front walls and she squinted.

"Goodbye, Penta. Come back at five." He waited stolidly for her to obey.

Her dignity had taken as much battering as she could handle. Her nose in the air, she swept out...and then spun on her toes to make one last plea.

For the second time in their short acquaintance, Cash shut a door in her face.

Cash didn't feel bad for forcing Penta Potter to leave. The lesson he intended to teach her son would be blunted if she bore some of the load, so she had to go. He understood why she was nervous. It wasn't like his appearance inspired confidence, especially in nice, sheltered women from upper middle-class backgrounds.

She didn't need to worry. He wasn't going to beat the kid. Unless he continued to disrespect his mother. Then the boy would earn a smack upside the head.

He couldn't help the inward bubble of hilarity whenever he thought of her name. *Penta Potter*. It belonged to a children's variety performer, not a lush mature woman with a full-lipped mouth, fiery brown eyes, and tangle of curly hair. Penta meant five in Latin or something, didn't it? He wondered why her parents had chosen it, and then wondered if she'd chosen it herself for a personal reason.

He wondered about her a lot as he and Cyril set the showroom to rights.

While he was a firm believer in making the punishment fit the crime, having the boy help was also a necessity. Absolute Motorcycle Repair was a one-man operation. The retail products he carried were just a sideline, a convenience for his customers. His main revenue came from restoring old bikes and maintaining new ones. People paid for Cash's expertise, not some flunky, so he'd never had the inclination or need to take on staff. Officially he was closed on Sundays, though he usually worked at least a few hours anyway. And on the rare—*extremely* rare—occasions he would be away for a day or more, he updated his website and answering machine and left a notice on the door. No one had ever objected.

Together, he and the teen gathered up the items that had been tossed from the shelves and separated them into two piles—one of goods that could be salvaged and one of those too damaged to sell, even at a discount. He probably should have left everything as it was until he'd talked to his insurance company, but he couldn't be bothered to wait. He'd put in a claim for the broken door and smashed windows and leave it at that.

Cyril worked in silence, his spine and shoulders stiff with protest. Since his complaints went unspoken, Cash chose to ignore the glares occasionally shot his way. He knew it was embarrassment more than fear that kept the boy quiet and was okay with that. The humiliation was part of the lesson the teen needed to learn.

They were interrupted a few times by customers dropping in. Cash helped those he could, but most he sent away for the time being. All of them expressed shock at the devastation and many studied Cyril with open curiosity. Cash offered only the briefest of details and refused to explain the boy's presence.

Just after noon, he was wondering if he could trust Cyril to stick around if he went to grab them burgers when the door opened once more. He looked up from examining the Gold Wing that had been knocked to the ground. A young woman stood silhouetted by the sunlight, poker straight blond hair streaming over her shoulders. Most of his customers were balding middle-aged men.

Making sure the bike was steady on its kickstand, he went to greet her. "Can I help you?"

She stared at him, blue eyes uncertain as she fidgeted with the hem of a belly-baring sweater. "Are you Cash? Cash Rylance?"

He nodded. There was something vaguely familiar about her. She was younger than he'd first thought, mid-teens probably. A scattering of acne reddened the skin on her forehead. Had she come to pick up an order for someone?

Her lip trembled and she lifted her chin with an odd sideways jerk. The gesture sparked a deeply hidden memory. His gut twisted. Hard.

"I'm Elle Stornaway," she said with defiance. "Linda's my mom. And you're my dad."

Chapter Three

"What are you doing here?" The words burst from Cash, propelled by shock and dismay.

Elle flinched but stood her ground. "To meet you."

"No." Dread surged through his veins, snapping with vicious teeth. She was going to ruin *everything*.

Again with the lifted chin. Linda made exactly the same motion when she was being stubborn. "You're my dad. I deserve to know you."

"I'm not worth knowing." When he'd been released from jail he'd made two vows—never to go back inside and to protect the daughter he'd never seen. Even though it meant cutting her out of his life, he'd kept those vows for twelve years and fully intended to keep them until the end of his days. "Go home. Does your mother know you're here?"

Her eyelids flickered. "She thinks I'm with friends."

Great. Linda was going to be furious. He and his ex-girlfriend had a pact. He kept his distance, and she sent him an update every year on their daughter's birthday. Usually it was a terse, bare bones email— text only, no photos. He never complained, grateful for any scraps she was willing to share. The next message was due in two weeks and three days.

Yearning seared his heart. He had to send Elle away, but since she was here...

"How did you find me?"

Colour rose in her cheeks. "Mom always said she'd

tell me about my dad when I was older. Well, I'm almost sixteen. I said if she didn't tell me now, I wouldn't live with her anymore. I'd go to Gramma and Gramps or stay with Shelby's family."

The news just got better and better. Cash squeezed his eyes shut briefly. Who the hell was Shelby? Linda would lay *that* at his door too. "You shouldn't have threatened her."

Elle shifted her feet, sneakers squeaking on the concrete floor. "Yeah, maybe. But she *promised* me."

He sincerely doubted Linda had promised to tell Elle anything. But to a child wondering about her father, he imagined any words other than a flat out "no" could be twisted into a commitment to tell the truth in the future.

A cell phone rang. Elle fished one out of the back pocket of her jeans and looked at Cash with anxious eyes. "Mom."

"Don't tell her where you are." Perfect. Now he was encouraging his daughter to lie. But what good would it do to tell the truth? "Say you're on the way home. Because you are. You have to go. I mean it."

Silence expanded between them, punctured by four more shrill rings before the call dropped.

"You're my dad." Elle's eyes glistened with tears. "I want to get to know you. I *need* to get to know you."

He shook his head, a granite weight of sorrow and regret bowing his neck. "Trust me on this. It's better if you don't. Go home, Elle. Have a good life. But don't come back."

Grief and pain etched her smooth young face and gave him a glimpse of what she'd look like in maturity. With a sob she spun around, pushed hard on the door, and vanished onto the sidewalk.

The plywood-covered frame swung back into place, darkening the interior to a shade as ashy as his soul. He stood frozen, staring forward as if he could still see her, wishing he could have given a different answer. Wishing a lot of things in his life were different.

"That was a shit thing to do."

He'd forgotten Cyril was there. He turned to the boy, who gripped a large push broom, a pile of glass shards at his feet.

His Adam's apple bobbed in his skinny neck. "I mean it. She was scared, coming to meet you for the first time. And you were a jerk."

There was nothing wrong with the boy's nerve. Cash gave him credit for standing up for Elle. Didn't mean he had to tolerate it.

"Mind your own business." He put as much menace in his voice as he could and was sourly pleased to see Cyril take a small step back. "Dustpan's in the storeroom. Go get it. Now."

Cyril was waiting on the sidewalk outside Absolute Motorcycle Repair when Penta arrived to pick him up. She told herself she was relieved not to have to face Cash again. That's what that twinge was. Relief, not disappointment. How could she be disappointed at *not* seeing a scary, bearded, tattooed biker?

Once on their way, she asked how the day had gone. Cyril merely grunted.

"Are you finished? Is everything cleaned up?" she prodded.

He sighed, the long-suffering sigh of a teenager wishing he were anywhere but trapped in a car with his annoying mother. "Most of it. He says I've still got to work off the cost of damages. He told me to go back Monday after school."

Irritation flared, infinitely more welcome than the unsettling attraction she'd experienced earlier. Who did Cash Rylance think he was? It was Penta's responsibility to discipline her children. Wasn't a day of unpaid labour enough? She squelched the disturbing memory of the ransacked showroom, along with the sinking suspicion that Cyril owed Cash whatever the stern-faced man demanded.

"You have track and field then." It was the one activity Cyril hadn't abandoned after the divorce, and she wanted nothing to jeopardize that tiny ray of normalcy. "Did you tell him you couldn't come?"

Cyril shrugged. Whatever that meant.

It was Penta's turn to sigh. "Never mind. I'll take care of it."

Which was why, on Monday afternoon at three-thirty, she was the one opening the still plywood-covered door at Cash's shop and stepping inside.

The showroom looked much better than the first time she'd seen it. Many of the shelves were bare and the whole place had a rather naked appearance, but it was neat and tidy. In the far corner, where rows of mysterious tools hung from metal pegboards above scarred wooden worktops, a rusted, battered motorcycle was surrounded by discarded bits and pieces that gave evidence of work in progress.

No one was in sight, though she could hear movement through the door that led to the back of the building. She drifted toward the bike. It wasn't just poorly cared for. It was ancient, even to her untutored eye. Nothing like the two gleaming monsters at the front of the shop with their ergonomically padded seats, mirror-like chrome, and complicated dashboards.

Motorcycles rarely crossed her mind, other than as machines whose riders were obviously courting certain death. But during the last planning session of the Silverberry Book Club, the group had decided one of their outings would be an introductory learn-to-ride course. It was scheduled for a week tomorrow. And here she was, surrounded by bikes, their maintenance supplies, and other related paraphernalia.

Coincidences made her edgy. The thought that uncontrollable fate might be directing her life was even more disturbing.

Cash Rylance appeared in the inner doorway carrying a cardboard box about the size of a large microwave. He scowled. "Where's Cyril?"

Well, hello to you too. "He has track and field after school on Monday, so I've come in his place."

The creases between Cash's brows deepened. An oil-stained red and black bandanna kept his hair off his forehead, the skin there marked by a rust-coloured streak. "I told you. This is Cyril's responsibility, not yours. Go home." He strode to the worktop and lowered the box. He wore another short-sleeved T-shirt, this one black with a large skull screen-printed on the back, and jeans that were more holes than fabric.

She caught a glimpse of a hairy, taut, thick thigh, swallowed, and scrambled to form a reply. "He's just a boy. I agree he deserves punishment. Which is why I've grounded him for a month except for school activities."

"And coming here. More days he skips, longer it'll take. No skin off my nose." He faced her, leaned a hip against the counter, and crossed his arms. The tattoos between his elbows and wrists rippled as long muscles and tight tendons flexed. "He has to work off his debt himself. Won't learn anything if you protect him by doing it for him."

"I'm not protecting him. I just told you. He's grounded."

"How do you know he's not going to sneak out of the house and meet his buddies anyway?"

Until this past weekend, she would have stoutly rejected the idea of Cyril doing any such thing. But since that was exactly what he had done...

She hadn't yet come up with a response when the front door swung open, sweeping sunlight across the concrete floor. A shrill female voice slashed the air.

"Stay away from Elle, Cash. I'm warning you!"

***Goddamn it. What** is Linda doing here?*

Cash had spent much of Sunday waiting for his ex to appear in this exact way...an avenging fury intent on mayhem. When she hadn't, he'd begun to hope Elle had kept the truth from her mother.

So much for that.

Linda stormed past Penta like she wasn't there, stopping only when she was toe to toe with him. "You swore you would never go near her, Cash. You *swore*."

"I didn't." It was a weak protest, but he had to make it. "She approached me. *She* came to *my* shop."

Linda waved that away. The blond hair she'd bequeathed to their daughter was piled in a messy bun on top of her head instead of hanging straight and smooth, and the same blue eyes snapped with mature displeasure instead of wavering with teenage uncertainty. Otherwise, the resemblance was uncanny. "You should have told me she came. I had to worm it out of her inch by inch. I *knew* she wasn't with friends. I *knew* it."

He resisted the urge to squirm. She was right. He should have told her. But he hadn't wanted to rat Elle out. He'd wanted his daughter to know she could trust him, at least in this instance.

Linda didn't wait for his response. She poked his shoulder. "You know what she did? She threatened to move out of the house if I didn't tell her who her father was. I had to give in. I didn't want to, but I had to." The fury in her voice was laced with unshed tears. "Now she's threatening to go if I don't let her visit again."

"I told her to get out. I told her she shouldn't have come." He wanted to rub his chest, where an unrelenting ache had throbbed all of Elle's life, but didn't move. Impossible to ignore even when she was unaware of his existence, it had intensified since his first sight of her.

She'd defied her mother to meet him. Was that a sign he'd paid his debt?

No. It was best for everyone if life stayed the way it was. Spending time with Elle would be dangerous, and not just to his peace of mind. To her safety. He knew too many bad people, people he didn't want near her. When he'd left prison, he'd done his best to make a clean break, avoid anyone from his past, anyone that might drag him back into the life he had led before. But the only thing he was good at was fixing motorcycles and, when old buddies had appeared, eager to have him work on their bikes again, he couldn't afford to refuse. It had been that or not eat.

Linda's next words echoed his thoughts. "I don't want Elle exposed to your kind of life, Cash. To gangs and drugs and bikers. She's so smart. She writes poetry that makes you cry and wants to go to university. I won't let you jeopardize that. If you had walked away from it all, had put your past behind you, maybe I'd think differently. But you got out of jail and went straight back to your old job, your old clients. My daughter deserves better."

Our daughter, he protested. But only in his head. He nodded.

Linda drew in a deep breath, searched his face, and seemed reassured by whatever she read there. Her shoulders lowered a fraction. "Okay, then." She took two steps backward. "Okay. Goodbye, Cash."

Again without any sign she'd seen Penta, she crossed the room and left.

Chapter Four

Penta should have slipped out when the blond woman began berating Cash. But it had happened so quickly she'd barely had time to comprehend what was going on before it was over.

The silence after the angry woman stormed out was as brittle as cracked crystal. Penta inhaled and exhaled in shallow sips, afraid too deep a breath would shatter the calm.

Cash smoothed his beard in a casual gesture that was belied by the suppressed tension humming around him. And though his expression was flat and unreadable, his gaze arrowed over Penta's shoulder in the direction of the door like a heat-seeking missile locked onto its target.

With a suddenness that made her jolt, he straightened, turned his back, and continued their conversation as if there had been no interruption. "Bring Cyril tomorrow and Wednesday." Picking up a wrench, he replaced it on the pegboard and reached for another tool. Penta had the distinct impression ingrained habit had taken over and he wasn't aware of what he was doing. "I'm still totalling the damages. So far, he owes me at least a hundred hours based on the minimum wage. Figure out a schedule. Let me know when he'll be here."

She stared at his set shoulders. His motions were harsh and jerky, as if he wasn't quite in control of his muscles. She didn't know him, but if she had to guess, she'd say he was *hurting*.

The woman's diatribe had been a flood of facts that Penta was only now absorbing.

Cash had been to jail.

He had a daughter he had agreed not to see.

That daughter had recently appeared at his shop.

The girl's mother was furious and terrified.

Sympathy tugged her in opposing directions. Penta could completely understand the other mother's need to protect her daughter. Yet, the man was in obvious pain. Despite the fact his appearance did not instill confidence, he hadn't done anything sinister in her presence.

Threading her way past the bike, she came to a halt at his elbow. His gaze remained abstracted as he rubbed a grimy rag on the pitted wooden top. The scent of oil and grease mingled with pine. She laid a tentative hand on his forearm, the flesh warm and vibrant beneath her palm. She'd half expected to be able to feel his tattoo under her fingertips, but of course she couldn't.

"I'm sorry." She said it softly, the way she would if one of her children had had their heart stomped on. He stopped wiping, his arm tensing and flexing though no longer moving back and forth. Too shy to look at him directly, she kept her eyes down. "I don't know what that was all about, but it obviously upset you."

He remained silent.

She patted his arm and stepped back. "Cyril will be here by three-thirty tomorrow. I'll pick him up at five-thirty, so he has time for dinner and homework. I'll also email you a schedule for the rest of his hours."

Cash nodded.

When she closed the door behind her, he was standing in his workspace, his back to the door, hands pressed onto the counter, head bowed.

Penta dropped a grumbling Cyril off on Tuesday as promised. She didn't go into the shop, telling herself it was because there was no need, but knowing it also side-stepped any awkwardness lingering after the scene she'd witnessed. Cash didn't seem the kind of guy who appreciated being caught at a disadvantage. He probably never wanted to see her again. A stab of regret tickled her throat at the thought.

Somewhere in between daily visits to her widowed father, chauffeuring Abra to dance lessons, assisting at Delilah's soccer practices, and making meals only Felix thanked her for, she drafted Cyril's schedule. One hundred hours was a lot to fit between end of season track and field events and studying for final exams. No matter how she arranged it, she couldn't avoid his sentence stretching into July. She emailed it to Cash and received a terse acknowledgment of receipt in return.

She told Mark about Cyril's misdemeanors when he called to discuss weekend visits. Maybe she should have mentioned it sooner, but she avoided talking to her ex as much as she could.

"The little rat." Mark's tone was disappointed but not surprised. They'd discussed Cyril many times since their separation and shared concerns about their son's recent choices. "I'll have a talk with him."

"That would be good." Cyril had always listened to his father more than her. It rankled, but it was the truth, and she'd learned to accept it. "You'll pick him up from Absolute on Friday, keep him overnight, and bring him back Saturday to do his next shift?" She hoped he would spend quality time with Cyril, and not be distracted by his second family.

Mark had stunned her when he'd asked for a divorce. Would it have been easier to accept if he'd fallen in love with someone else? But that hadn't been the case. He'd simply wanted out.

He'd blamed it on her focus on their children. "You don't see me," he'd explained, "and I can't live like that any longer. I want a wife, not just a mother for my kids."

Which made it even more humiliating that, when he chose a new partner last year, she was a woman a couple years older than Penta with two teenage children of her own. She hadn't even been replaced by a younger model. She'd been swapped for a more outgoing, adventurous version of herself. One that went on solo vacations, belonged to clubs and committees, and had figured out how to raise her sons and still give Mark all the attention he thought he deserved.

She tuned back into the conversation.

"Yeah," Mark said. "And you can be sure he won't be sneaking out of my house."

She bristled. "Are you blaming me?"

"You baby the boy, Pen. You baby all of them. How will they ever respect you if you're constantly giving in to their demands?"

It was an old argument. So old it shouldn't bother her anymore, yet it did. She ignored it, confirmed the rest of the weekend's arrangements, and hung up.

Cyril's penance on Saturday was expected to end at five o'clock. Penta pulled up outside the shop a few minutes before the hour, parked, and tapped her fingers on the wheel with indecision. She had no reason to go in. But she was curious as to how things were going with Cash, and she'd never get a straight answer from her recalcitrant son. With a rising sense of expectation out of all proportion to her errand, she pushed open the van door.

As she stepped onto the road, a familiar SUV pulled in behind and Mark exited from the driver's side.

"What are you doing here?" Her question came out more accusatory than she'd meant it to.

Mark's face screwed up in a scowl. "Cyril's staying with me tonight. Didn't he tell you?"

Cash remembered being a teenage boy. He remembered being angry and confused and horny. He didn't remember being sullen and silent, but if Cyril was a typical example of the species, he must have been.

Not that Cash wanted him to be chatty. He was used to working alone and appreciated quiet. Still, Cyril exhibited a whole new level of closed-mouthedness, though it was amazing what the boy could communicate with a single grunt.

He was also a decent worker. He did what he was told without unnecessary questions and rarely had to be corrected or closely supervised. Underneath that morose, rebellious exterior was a good kid. Right now, he was sitting on a tall stool beside the workbench, going through a box of odds and ends, sorting the pieces into small containers while listening to something on his phone through earbuds.

Cash straightened from his crouch next to the classic '67 Triumph he was restoring. His knees creaked and his back ached as if in sympathy with the sorrowful-looking Baby Bonnie, which had been discovered abandoned, ignored, and neglected in a barn. The descendants of the recently deceased eighty-three-year-old woman who owned the ramshackle farm had practically paid him to take it away, overwhelmed by the task of dismantling a long life and not interested in his explanation of the Bonnie's potential value. When it was done it would be a beaut, but it was a demanding project and would take months to complete.

He wasn't sure what he'd do when it was finished. He'd make a pretty penny if he decided to sell but couldn't stifle the desire to keep it for himself. Not that he needed another bike. His first year out of prison, when he'd been rebuilding his business, he'd done major work on a 2003 Harley Road King Classic. The customer hadn't been able to pay and signed it over instead. He probably should have sold it, because he'd needed the money more than he'd needed the bike. But he hadn't, and speed-filled hours on the machine had saved his sanity more than once. It was lucky Cyril and his vandalizing buddies hadn't found it in the small lockup at the back of the shop. If they'd damaged it, who knew what he might have done?

He wiped his hands on a rag and flapped it in the teen's line of vision. Cyril flicked him a glance, tapped the screen of his phone to pause whatever was playing, and continued sorting.

"You're done," Cash said. "You can get back to it Tuesday."

A shrug was the only indication the boy had heard. He finished the bits and bobs in his palm, slid off the stool, tucked the containers under the workbench, and made his way to the room in the back where his jacket and backpack were stored.

The front door opened and two people walked in, silhouetted against the sunshine washing the sidewalk. Cash couldn't wait for the new glass to be installed next week. Not being able to see out onto the street was giving him prison flashbacks. Between nightmares he was back inside and restless dreams about his daughter, he hadn't slept well for a while. Not that he ever slept deeply.

Even before the door closed, he recognized Penta. Her curly brown hair and comfortably rounded body loosened something in his chest—and tightened something else lower down. He'd always been drawn to women with—as his mother would have said—meat on their bones. In the past, those women had worn tight jeans and blouses that strained at the buttons, not the roomy pants and oversized hoodies that seemed to be Penta's preferred wardrobe.

The man was dressed in the suburban dad's weekend outfit of jeans and short-sleeved polo shirt. He had the soft, puffy look of someone who spent most of his time behind a desk. His pinched mouth and creased forehead did nothing to change Cash's impression of a pompous man dissatisfied with life—his least favourite kind of client.

Ignoring him for the moment, Cash dipped his chin to Penta. "Cyril will be right out."

She opened her mouth, but the man spoke before she had a chance to say anything. "He's coming with me, actually." He stepped forward and held out a hand. "Mark Potter. Cyril's dad. Pen told me about the trouble our son caused you."

"Mark's my ex-husband." Penta's voice was breathless, her whiskey-brown eyes wide. Her hands gripped each other, flexing and relaxing.

Cash hadn't forgotten she was divorced. He hadn't forgotten anything she'd said to him. He shook Mark's hand, resisting the impulse to squeeze tighter than necessary.

"Cyril was supposed to let his mom know there was a change in plans. Should have known better than to trust a kid." Mark's laughter was bluff and hearty. Cash felt another ruffle of irritation, this time in defense of Cyril. "I figured it would be better if he spent a couple more nights with his dad. Get some man-to-man time. Pen's a good mom, but she's a little soft sometimes. Goes too easy on the kids."

Despite the fact Cash had thought the same thing, hearing the other man say it made him want to punch him in the nose, especially when Penta squirmed and studied the floor as if embarrassed. His own mother had been exhausted from working two jobs and any spare time she had was spent with her nose in a bottle, not with her only child. In his opinion, Penta's overprotectiveness was much better than the alternative. "You say that like it's a bad thing."

She lifted her gaze from the concrete and stared at him, shock evident in the rounded O of her mouth.

Mark raised an eyebrow and huffed another insincere laugh. "You've got a champion, have you, Pen?" He raked Cash from head to toe and quirked his mouth dismissively. "Not exactly your type."

"What does that mean?" Cash straightened his spine, squared his shoulders, and shifted his stance, looming over the other man.

And immediately felt ridiculous. Mark had said nothing but the truth. Cash wasn't a member of Penta's world, and never would be. It didn't matter that he was attracted to her. He couldn't imagine a universe in which Penta would be attracted to *him*, an ex-con biker mechanic.

Before he could make the situation worse, Cyril emerged from the back. *Thank Christ.*

His step hitched when he saw his parents. "Oh. Yeah, right."

"Yeah, right, indeed." Penta's smile was overly bright, her tone a fraction too tolerant. It seemed he wasn't the only one happy at the interruption. "Your dad says you were supposed to let me know the change in plans."

Cyril resumed his path to the exit without comment, and Cash's irritation flared again. Did *anyone* in Penta's family treat her with respect? He blocked the boy's escape with an outstretched arm. "Apologize to your mother. It's the least you can do for letting her make a trip for no reason."

"Fine. Sorry." Cyril slung his backpack over his shoulder and circled past the adults. "I'll be in the car."

Chapter Five

Penta watched Cyril leave, emotions tumbling like bricks from a badly built wall.

She hated that Mark had the power to make her feel like a poor mother, especially since he blamed their divorce on her parenting. Maybe she had let her confrontation-avoiding tendencies take the lead since then. Maybe she was a little lenient. Who cared? She had to make up for the cataclysm in her children's lives somehow.

"Guess that's my cue." Mark ambled after Cyril. "I'll get him to school on Monday. Then he's back with you."

She nodded mechanically, aware of Cash standing just behind her shoulder like a menacing sentinel. The door closed and they were alone.

Which was just a different kind of awkward. The look of derision in his eyes when Mark and then Cyril had dismissed her was branded on her retinas and his defense had only made her feel pitiful and angry. She should be able to stand up for herself. She certainly didn't want him to feel sorry for her. She wanted him to see her as—

—nope, not going there. Mark had been right about that, too, which was even more annoying. Cash wasn't her type. Her least favourite romances were the ones that paired the bad boy with the good girl. To Penta, that was simply a recipe for disaster.

"You okay?"

She turned, her arm brushing his as she did so. Even through the thick fabric of her sweatshirt, she could feel the heat of his skin and she shuffled backward quickly. "Of course. Why wouldn't I be? It was just a silly miscommunication." She was babbling again. Clamping her teeth together, she grinned at him, hoping it didn't look as insane as it felt.

His dark red eyebrows lowered. "I don't like your husband."

"Ex-husband." It was important Cash knew Mark meant nothing to her, though she didn't stop to examine why. "As ex as you can get."

"Right. You told me before. Twice, actually." His expression relaxed and a tiny twinkle shone in the steel of his irises.

That twinkle lit sparks low in her belly. Sparks she hadn't felt in a long time. In a desperate attempt to ignore them, she said the first thing that came to mind. "Why don't you like him? He was perfectly polite to you."

"Yes. To *me*."

The weight he put on the final word spoke volumes. Her cheeks flared with embarrassed heat.

He tilted his head to one side and studied her as if she were a creature he'd never seen before. "Do you want to get a coffee?"

She gawked. "A coffee? Me? With you?"

His lips pressed together, and his expression shuttered. "Never mind."

She thought back to her first sight of him—when she'd only known him as Big, Red, and Scary. The first two still applied, but she realized it wasn't fear that caused her skin to tingle when he was around. It was arousal. She might be a forty-four-year-old mother of four, but she wasn't dead.

However, there were a couple things she needed to clear up.

"Who was the blond woman? The one who came here and yelled at you."

Muscles in his jaw flexed. "Linda. We were together years ago. We broke up before our daughter was born."

She'd suspected something of the sort, but it was good to have confirmation. Now it was time for the biggie.

"What did you go to jail for?" The question had gnawed at her ever since the uncomfortable altercation she'd witnessed.

"Assault causing bodily harm." He met her stare directly. "It was a fight in a bar. The other guy started it, but I finished it. I've been out for twelve years."

She swallowed. How could she even contemplate going out for coffee with him? Mind you, she was probably reading more into a simple invitation than he intended. He couldn't be interested in her as a *woman*. He just felt sorry for her.

He was also the first person to ask her out for any reason at all since her divorce. She met plenty of single men—several of the fathers of her children's friends were also divorced—but none of them ever looked her way.

"Where should we go?" she asked.

They ended up at Café Voltaire. Penta drove her minivan and Cash followed on his bike.

He had never been to the trendy coffee shop attached to a local bookstore. Light glinted off the piercings in the barista's eyebrow and lip, and her tank top revealed several tattoos, but he was still glad he'd thrown a jacket over his T-shirt so most of his ink was hidden.

He regretted many things in his life, including several of the marks he'd had drawn on his body. Like his past, though, they were something he had no choice but to accept.

Penta insisted on buying his drink. He stuck with black coffee while she went for something that involved steaming and frothing and a sprinkle of dark chocolate on the resulting concoction. After they took their seats, she spent an inordinate amount of time fussing with the whipped cream streaking down the sides of the glass mug and avoiding his eyes.

"Are you wishing you hadn't come?" Her initial dismay at his invite had stabbed a raw spot he'd thought long since armoured and protected. When she'd said yes, he'd allowed himself a moment of joy before stamping it into submission.

He probably shouldn't have asked her. But she'd looked so forlorn he'd wanted to do something to cheer her up and figured his preferred release of a fast and frantic ride on two wheels down the highway wasn't an option.

"No." Her chin lifted at a defiant angle. "I'm being silly."

"It's not silly to worry about spending time with a guy that's been to jail."

Her brow creased. "You think that's my problem?"

"Isn't it?"

She shook her head, brown curls dancing. She'd held them back with a black band, so the strands were smooth around her face and the rest a riot of ringlets. "I wouldn't have come if that was an issue. I'm not that spineless." The last word spit from her lips like she'd taken a sip of something bitter.

"What's with the face, then?"

She didn't pretend to misunderstand. "Just thinking about Cyril. And Mark."

"Ah." He sipped his own drink. "I never did answer your question."

She stopped the spoonful of cream enroute to her mouth. "What question?"

"Why I don't like your *ex*-husband." He was careful to emphasize the distinction. "I didn't like the way he treated you."

The spoon slipped in and out of her full lips, and he had to look away for a moment. He'd devised ways to control his urges through the long nights of prison and the lonely years since. Penta, however, was constantly testing the limits of his endurance.

"He's right, you know. That's what makes it so maddening. I am too easy on the kids. It's a terribly hard balance at the best of times, and since the divorce—" She blocked whatever she'd been going to say with another mouthful of white foam.

Hopefully, she'd be done with the spoon soon. Otherwise, he was going to be *very* uncomfortable.

"Was he also right about me not being your type?" If she laughed and agreed, maybe his erection would get the hint.

She did laugh, but it was the saddest he'd ever heard. "That wasn't a dig at *you*. He was pointing out how boring I am. It was one of the reasons he asked for—" Again she cut herself off.

He could fill in the rest. "Now I *really* don't like him. Being sweet and loving and tender doesn't make you boring."

"It doesn't exactly make me a sex symbol, either." Her dry tone might have been an attempt at humour, but he heard the wistfulness behind it.

He reached across the table and ran his finger over the knuckles of her hand. "Sex symbols are overrated. I'd rather be with someone nice."

He'd meant it as a compliment, but her downturned mouth and averted gaze told him she'd missed his point. "*Nice*. That's worse than being boring."

The half-formed idea that had snuck into his thoughts after Linda's visit took a clearer shape. He pressed his fingers to her chin, encouraging her to lift her head and look at him. "Do you want to be a bad girl, Penta?"

Penta sat, frozen, as Cash swept her top lip with his broad thumb, his fingertips points of fire on her jaw.

After showing her the foam he'd wiped off, he slipped the digit into his mouth. She hoped he didn't hear the tiny moan she couldn't suppress. Waves of sensuality swept over her, flushing her skin, shortening her breath.

"Well? Want to be a bad girl?"

She watched his lips move. She'd never kissed anyone with such a lush beard. Dazed, she looked away from his mouth as she considered his question. Unfortunately, that just meant she was slammed by the full-on view. He sprawled on the hard wooden chair, one arm draped on the back, regarding her with lazy amusement.

She had never been a rebel. Never wanted to be one. But she *wanted* to be bad with Cash. Wanted it very, *very* much. Yet...

"What do you mean?" Her throat was so tight the words squeaked.

"You want to prove to your ex you're not boring? Maybe make him wish he hadn't left you?"

"I don't want him back, if that's what you're wondering." Mark had crushed her when he'd asked for a divorce. He'd accused her of ignoring him, of being unable to balance their children's needs with his, of being unexciting and unadventurous, in bed and out. She couldn't forgive him for that and would never risk that humiliation again.

"Doesn't mean you don't want to tweak his tail a little."

She wanted to do more than tweak his tail. She wanted to cut it off and feed it to him with a rake. Shocked at her own wish for revenge, especially so many years after the divorce, she stayed silent.

"Going out with me would show him exactly how much you've moved on."

"What would you get out of it?" He couldn't be interested in her, not *that* way. And he couldn't dislike Mark that much, not on such short acquaintance. What was his end game?

"I want to see more of my daughter." His voice was harsh with longing. "Linda believes I'm a dangerous influence. But Elle is growing up and I'm afraid she's going to make bad choices if Linda continues to block her. Maybe if she thinks I'm dating you—a stable, responsible, suburban mom—that will ease her fears."

She couldn't help feeling slightly deflated by his prosaic explanation, but he had to like her at least a little if he was suggesting such a deception.

"It would all be a ruse, though." She wanted to make sure she understood the rules. "You'd be the bad boy to my bad girl with Mark, and I'd be the good girl to your good boy with Linda. Once you've improved your standing with her and I've had my fun teasing him, we'd end it?"

He nodded. "Exactly."

She bit her lip. "I need to think about it."

"Of course." He drained his coffee and stood up. "You know where to find me."

Chapter Six

Penta thought of little else for the next few days. At times, she was ready to snap up Cash's proposal like a trout sighting a shiny, sharp lure. At others, she berated herself for not shutting down the idea the moment he mentioned it.

While she wouldn't mind flaunting a sexy, bad-ass boyfriend to her staid, slightly paunchy ex, she'd confessed the truth when she told Cash she didn't want to reconcile with Mark. He'd burned too many bridges during their painful separation and divorce. Even if he approached her on bended knee—which she couldn't imagine, not in a million years—she wouldn't take him back.

No, her main reason for accepting Cash's challenge would be because she wanted to. It would give her the chance to rebel in safety. Because as dangerous as Cash looked, she knew instinctively he'd never hurt her.

Do you want to be a bad girl, Penta?

How did one become a bad girl? she wondered. Was it a gift at birth? Or was it achievable through practice?

By the time Tuesday evening arrived, she was no closer to deciding.

Leaving Delilah overseeing Abra's homework and Felix keeping a clandestine eye on Cyril, she set out for the fairground parking lot where the Silverberry Book Club was gathering for their June meeting. Normally she looked forward to their monthly get-together. Tonight, however, they were being introduced to riding motorcycles. It would be impossible to forget Cash and his tempting proposition while surrounded by the machines he pampered.

She pulled into a slot and surveyed the course laid out in orange cones with trepidation. The huge parking lot was empty except for a few vehicles she recognized as belonging to club members, a shiny black pickup with a large, enclosed trailer attached— both sporting the logo of the driving school—and three motorbikes propped up on kickstands.

Helen Mansfield, the matriarch of the Silverberries, and her husband, Nathan Spieth, stood chatting with Terrance Renfrew and Natalie Minton in a loose huddle near the bikes. Penta climbed out of her van and went to join them.

"Hello, all." She included everyone in her wave, creasing her cheeks into a smile she hoped signalled excitement, not distress. "Ready to risk death and dismemberment?"

"I don't think it will come to that," Helen replied, grinning. The older woman was the kind of person Penta wanted to be when she grew up—confident, independent, and fearless. "You could have used your veto if you're that concerned. Come to think of it, have you ever used it?"

"No." Penta had joined the Silverberry Book Club after her separation because it pushed her out of her comfort zone. Using her veto would have defeated that purpose.

Terrance nudged her with his elbow. "Penta's our secret wild child, isn't she?"

His teasing touched an exposed nerve given her Cash conundrum, but she kept her voice light and level. "I just don't want to disappoint anyone."

"That I believe." They'd been instructed to wear heavy footwear, long-sleeved shirts, and jeans. Terrance had followed the rules, though his denim was precisely pressed and his shirt a crisp green button down. A thin fine scarf in matching hues was knotted neatly around his neck.

While she considered all the Silverberries friends, she and Terrance had developed a special bond. On lonely nights she wondered if it might have led to a deeper relationship—if he hadn't been gay. And married.

Glancing around, she asked no one in particular, "Where's our instructor?"

As if conjured by her question, a man stepped down the ramp sloping from the end of the trailer. He wore a black leather jacket and carried a stack of clipboards.

Cash.

Cash enjoyed Penta's gob-smacked expression rather more than he suspected he should. It was a small payback for keeping him on tenterhooks for days. The longer he waited for her decision, the more he regretted his proposal. The delay obviously meant she was going to say no. He wished she'd get it over with.

While he was a certified motorcycle instructor, he didn't offer classes through his own business. To keep his hand in, he occasionally helped out a buddy who did. Jesse had called him a few weeks ago.

"I got an odd request," he had explained. "This woman asked if I could do a customized introductory course for her book club. Nothing official, just a casual demonstration-type thing. No one's ever wanted anything like that before, but I figured what the hell."

Cash was sure he'd misheard. "Book club?"

"Yeah. She said something about not really being a book club anymore. I didn't get into it. Who cares what they call themselves as long as they pay in advance. I'll email you the list of students and waivers and other shit you need a couple days before."

Which was when Cash had discovered Penta was one of the participants.

He jerked his chin in her direction but gave no indication they'd met. He had no idea how she'd choose to play this and would let her take the lead. Not everyone wanted to admit they knew a motorcycle-riding ex-con. If she pretended he was a stranger, that was fine.

Which was total bullshit. It would rip him up if she ignored him.

He scanned the group. "Helen?"

The grey-haired woman beamed at him, eyes bright with enthusiasm. "That's me. You must be Cash."

He checked the signup sheet. "I have seven students listed. We waiting for the rest?"

"I'm sure they'll be here soon."

He nodded. "Even though this is a modified class, Jesse wants all the usual paperwork filled out. Might as well get that started." He handed out the clipboards he'd prepared, leaving Penta to the last.

She took hers with a wide-eyed gaze. "Why didn't you mention you'd be our instructor?"

The fussily dressed man next to her slid them an interested glance. Cash ignored him. "I didn't know. Only got the names yesterday morning." If he'd told her, would she have come? Or would she have made an excuse to drop out.

"I see." She unclipped the pen he'd hooked onto each clipboard and immediately dropped it.

He retrieved it and held it out to her. She took it gingerly, avoiding any contact.

"Excuse me. Can you explain something?" With relief, he turned to answer the dark-haired woman's question.

The other two students—a tall, wide-shouldered woman with a confident stride and another woman with silvery-blond hair in a long ponytail—arrived. In the flurry of introductions, equipment explanations, and safety briefings, he had no further chance to talk with Penta privately.

He wasn't sure whether to be disappointed or relieved.

Penta's shoulders slumped as Cash turned to Natalie, the twanging tension tightening her tendons releasing now his focus had shifted.

"Tell all to Uncle Terrance." Her friend's brows peaked inquisitively, eyes flashing with curiosity. "How do you know our hot instructor? And how come you didn't tell me?"

"It's a long story." She stared at the form clipped to the board without taking in the printed words.

"He's rather luscious, isn't he?" Terrance kept his voice low. "I don't usually go for the burly, bearded types. But there's something about a dangerous man that...gets my motor revving, you might say."

"What would *Bennett* say if he heard you?" Penta had intended the question to be a joke and was surprised at how sharp it sounded in her own ears.

All the fun fled Terrance's expression. "He wouldn't care."

The dullness in his tone erased the exasperation his comment had sparked. "What do you mean? Is everything okay with you two?"

He shrugged. "We're just going through a sticky patch. Every couple does, right?" He turned his attention to his own clipboard, clearly indicating the subject was closed.

Anxiety over Terrance's marriage tugged at her until Cash directed the group to join him around the motorbikes. She paid close attention to his simple, clear instructions and his calm, confident air soothed her. Maybe, if he was the driver, she might possibly contemplate taking a ride. Someday. One far into the future.

He straddled the biggest bike, drawing up the

stand and settling into the seat with an easy grace that rippled awareness down her spine. He looked completely at home, his feet in their thick leather boots planted on either side as he balanced the heavy machine effortlessly. Her gaze lingered on how his big hands gripped the handlebars, the way his thighs flexed under his jeans.

And always, just below the surface of her conscious thoughts, shimmered the knowledge that she could pretend he was hers. If she was brave enough.

He was only offering a fake relationship, but it was the closest she'd get to being the wild child Terrance had laughingly called her. It was tempting. So tempting.

Everyone was invited to sit in the saddle and experiment with the controls—with the engine safely off. Penta was surprised at how comfortable the seat was and doubly thankful there was a machine suited for her shorter frame. She could imagine the hilarity if she crashed onto the pavement and was pinned underneath the chassis.

Cash explained correct postures and holds and provided advice in his deep, calm voice, moving from one Silverberry to the next with professional aplomb.

"Nice and gentle." He stood at her shoulder and watched as she squeezed the clutch lever. "Your grip should be firm but relaxed."

For some unexplainable reason, Penta's cheeks flared with heat. He leaned over and adjusted her hand on the black rubber throttle. Her mouth went dry.

"Smooth, even motions. Don't hold it too tightly." His breath fanned her cheek. A hint of coffee and spice wafted to her nose.

She resisted the urge to squirm, her thighs squeezing the seat between her legs involuntarily. He was doing it on purpose. He had to be.

Doing what exactly she refused to examine.

Toward the end of the session, Cash offered to take each of them on a slow sedate ride around the temporary track laid out by the pylons. Confronted so soon with the opportunity she'd recently considered, Penta remained silent. Terrance rejected the idea outright, but the others accepted.

One by one, the Silverberries climbed up behind Cash and circled the short route. After Natalie slid off, pleased and excited, he turned to Penta. "What about you? Are you up for a ride?"

Again, she had the distinct impression his words held a double entendre. He was brash and bold, and she wanted to absorb that energy. In that instant, she made her decision about his unsettling proposal.

Answering with a double meaning of her own, she lifted her chin and met his gaze squarely. "Yes, I am."

Chapter Seven

Cash held himself stiffly as Penta buckled on a borrowed helmet and approached the bike. He'd teased her subtly all evening and enjoyed it, but now it was about to bite him in the ass.

"Put your foot on the peg so you can swing up." His voice was hoarse, and he cleared his throat.

She did so, shuffling back so there was a gap between their bodies.

"This bike has hand grips just under your hips. We won't be going fast so those should be enough, but, if you need to, you can hold onto me." He wanted her to take up his invitation more than he should, given the current state of their relationship. "Don't wriggle around or you might throw off the balance. When we go into a turn, lean the way I do." He turned his chin so he could see her out of the corner of his eye. "Any questions?"

She shook her head.

"Ready?"

A nod this time. He set the bike into motion and heard a quick inhalation.

Keeping the pace easy, he wound his way through the course. The occasional random brush of her thighs against his hips, her breasts against his back, ratcheted his pulse into top gear, and by the time he pulled to a stop near the trailer his body was thrumming with need.

She slid off the seat, stumbling a little. He reached

out to steady her and got his first good look at her face. Her full cheeks were shining, eyes sparkling.

"I did it." Her tone was full of wonder. "I thought I'd be more scared, but I wasn't. I kind of liked it."

An overwhelming inclination to tug her into his arms shocked him. He nodded curtly and rolled the bike a couple steps back. "Time to pack up."

He busied himself with collecting pylons, helmets, and other equipment and stowing it all inside the trailer. Penta and her friends gathered in a chattering group near their vehicles. Their obvious camaraderie ignited a familiar despair, and he kept his head down, concentrating on his work, doing his best to ignore the swamping isolation.

He strode down the ramp of the trailer to find Helen standing at the bottom. She'd removed her heavy long-sleeved shirt and draped it around her shoulders, revealing a tie-died tank top.

"I wanted to thank you." She glowed with delight, as she had all evening. He guessed she was about twenty years older than him, but her lust for life made her seem ageless. "We had such fun. I wouldn't be surprised if a couple of us signed up for the real course."

"Jesse will be glad to hear it." He strode to a bike, gripped the handles, and swept up the kickstand with his foot.

"We're all heading to the restaurant across the street for appies and drinks. One of our members recently had a baby and couldn't come to the lesson but is meeting us there." She pointed over the wide thoroughfare that edged the west side of the parking lot. "Why don't you join us?"

Just what he wanted. To be the odd man out in a group of longtime friends. "I gotta get back to the garage."

"I understand. Well, thanks for an awesome evening." She turned to go, hesitated, and then turned back. "Sorry. One more question." She reached out and touched the tattoo on his hand with a fingertip. "That's a beautiful design. Where did you get it?"

He stared at the phoenix. Its spread wings and proud head cover the back of his palm and wrist, with the feathers of its tail trailing down his fingers. Rendered in blacks and oranges and reds, it was dramatic and bold. "Golden Dragon." It was the only ink he'd had done since getting out of jail and one of the few he didn't regret.

Her nod was smug with satisfaction. "I thought I recognized Sven's work. He was a true artist."

He raised surprised eyebrows. "You knew Sven?" He scanned the skin visible on her neck and arms. No tattoos in sight. He knew all sorts of people were getting inked these days, yet he struggled to believe Helen had.

"I worked for him for a few years. When he retired, I bought the shop. Golden Dragon is mine now."

Appearances obviously could be deceiving. Except for himself. Shaving his beard and wearing clothing that had fewer skulls and grease stains might make him more presentable, but that would only be a cosmetic change. He was who he was, and the world needed to be warned. Like his tattoos, his past was drawn in indelible ink.

Unfazed by his lack of response, Helen remained cheery and friendly. "Are you sure you can't come for a quick minute? We won't bite, I promise." She twinkled with mischievous glee, and he weakened, loneliness gnawing at his resolve.

Penta detached herself from the group by the vehicles and approached. She spoke to Helen. "Nathan says he's dying of thirst."

"Of course he is." Her tone was indulgent. She gave Cash another radiant smile. "If you change your mind, you know where to find us."

Penta didn't follow Helen when she returned to her husband and friends with brisk, lively steps. But she didn't look at Cash, either, just stared into the distance, fingers entwined in a hard knot at her waist.

He shrugged and rolled the bike into the trailer. He'd given up hope that she might accept his suggestion. After spending time with her friends, he realized how ridiculous the idea was. Her wish to revolt, to step out of her cozy life, had been the impulse of a moment. No way would she actually do it.

He anchored the bike in place, checked to make sure it was secure, and went back for the next one. Penta still stood there, watching the line of her friends' vehicles snake out of the parking lot and onto the road.

In silence, he gripped the handlebars and raised his foot to swipe at the stand.

"Okay. I'm in."

His head jerked toward her, vertebrae popping. "You are?"

She met his gaze, fear and resolve tangling in her expression. Her nod was quick and brittle.

He'd never felt this level of relief and anticipation before, not even the day he'd left prison. "You'll help me with Elle?"

"I will." Her lips flattened into a thin, determined line. "And you'll try to give me some street cred."

He couldn't help it. He burst out laughing.

Well, this is going swimmingly, Penta thought in sour frustration. Here she'd gathered her courage and jumped off the high diving board—

—only to be *laughed* at.

She spun on her toes and stalked toward her van.

"Penta! Wait." Heavy boots thudded behind her and a strong hand gripped her elbow.

It was an impersonal touch compared to being perched behind him on the motorbike. Then she'd been hyperaware of how he'd fit between her legs, how the strong column of his neck had been within nuzzling distance. Her belly bloomed with heat at the memory.

She yanked out of his grasp, halted her headlong rush, and swung to confront him. "You *laughed* at me!"

He held his palms out like shields. "I'm sorry. It wasn't *at* you. I promise."

"Oh, really?" She pinned him with the glare she used on her children when they lied to her.

Amazingly, it worked. He twitched a bulky shoulder in an odd shamefaced jerk. "Maybe a little. It was hearing you say street cred. But I'm really happy you agreed."

She searched his face and saw no mockery. Her annoyance ebbed. "You are?"

"I am." One hand reached as if to touch her. When he lowered his arm without making contact, disappointment shimmered across her shoulder blades.

Traffic whooshing by on the nearby road suddenly sounded unnaturally loud. The drone of a plane overhead made her nerves itch. She opened her mouth. Then closed it. Now she'd announced her decision, she had no idea what came next.

Cash seemed to have the same problem. He stood quietly, fingers combing through his beard. The longest day of the year was only two and a half weeks away and the sky was bright with sunlight at nine-thirty in the evening. Bronze and cinnamon sparks flared off his hair, completely uncovered for the first time since she'd met him. She'd wondered if he wore ball caps and kerchiefs to hide incipient baldness, but that wasn't the case. His skull was covered in thick strands of rich red shot through with glints of silver, cut short at the sides and a little longer on top. Combined with his abundant whiskers, he flared like a match, bright and dangerous.

She drew a shaky breath and managed two syllables. "Now what?"

He huffed a small chuckle. "I was so certain you were going to say no I didn't make any plans."

Her hackles rose again. "You didn't think I'd have the guts, did you?"

He balanced on his toes in a lithe, vaguely aggressive stance. "This isn't going to work if you get angry every time I open my mouth."

She'd almost forgotten how big and solid he was. That was how comfortable she'd gotten with him. She deflated. "You're right. I'm a little defensive, I guess."

"Porcupines are less prickly than you. Stop trying to read between the lines. I'm a blunt guy, Penta. I say what I mean."

"Got it." She shifted her weight, feeling unsettled and adrift. "I guess we should decide what to tell everyone. A cover story."

"What's wrong with the truth? We met because of Cyril. You can decide how much we share about that." He jerked a thumb over his shoulder in the direction of the restaurant across the street. "Helen invited me for a drink. If anyone asks, we say we decided to date after that. It's close enough to what really happened."

He made it sound so easy. "Okay."

"Want to help me load these?" He pointed at the bikes waiting to go in the trailer. "Then we can walk over together. It'll look good, help establish our story to your friends." His beard couldn't hide the gleam of his teeth, bared in an infectious grin.

"If you like." This levity was something she'd never seen in him before. She could only assume it was because she'd agreed to help him. Pleasure at being needed eased more of her nervousness.

She took a firm grip on the handlebars of the smallest bike. It was still heavy and awkward to maneuver. She prayed she wouldn't drop it. "We have our past and tonight figured out. But what about tomorrow?"

"There's no need to rush into things." He pushed his bike up the ramp's incline, and she followed, puffing with effort. "I've kept away from Elle for sixteen years. Another few days won't matter."

Kept away was an odd choice of words. She'd have to ask him to explain, but that could wait for now.

They worked in tandem to secure the bikes. Penta hesitated to broach how she would benefit from the deal. Cash yearned to connect with his only child but believed she was doing it as a lark, a safe way to pretend she was someone other than a plump, boring, middle-aged mother. From his point of view, her reasons must look frivolous and selfish.

An even more depressing thought followed. She had been that person for so long she wasn't sure she could be anyone else. But the older her children grew, the less they needed her. What would she do when they were adults and left her? Who would she be then?

Maybe this escapade with Cash could help her figure that out.

Cash locked the trailer, and they walked side-by-side across the parking lot without speaking. At the intersection, they waited decorously for the light to change, crossed the street, and made their way to the long low-roofed pub. Throughout the short journey, Penta fought a ridiculous wish to take his hand. Not as a ploy to convince her friends they were a couple, but for moral support. Faking a relationship was the most outrageous thing she'd ever done in her life. She needed all the encouragement she could get.

The sun had fallen below the hills to the west and a slight chill nipped the air. Outdoor heaters glowing with warmth were interspersed between high tables in a fenced-in patio that ran the length of the building. The Silverberries were seated at one long enough for the whole group. Penta was glad to see Lynn had managed to join them. Her friend had given birth in frantic fashion only two months ago. While she appeared healthy and happy, she had the wan, stretched-thin look of a forty-two-year-old woman with a preschooler and a newborn in desperate need of adult conversation.

They had to enter the bar in order to access the patio. The front door was around the corner and as soon as they were out of sight of the Silverberries, Penta came to an abrupt halt. "We need a safe word."

Cash's eyebrows shot to his hairline. "What do you know about safe words?"

Her cheeks heated. This man had made her blush more often in the last few hours than she had in years. "They're not only for sex. My kids and I chose safe words, in case I had to send someone they didn't know to get them from school."

The doors pushed open, and a noisy quartet exited. He waited for them to move out of hearing before he continued. "Why do you think we need one?"

"Until we set firmer boundaries about what this entails, we need to be able to alert the other if we're feeling uncomfortable."

His expression darkened. "If I ever make you uncomfortable, Penta, you just have to say so. You don't have to be secretive about it."

She toyed with the zipper on her hoodie, sliding it up and down in short, jerky movements, nervous energy overflowing in fidgets. "I was thinking more about you. I don't want to screw up your chance at getting to know your daughter. If I'm doing something you don't like or worry that Linda won't like, you need to let me know, without risking our..." She searched for a word that described the situation best and came up blank.

He stared at her like he'd never seen her before. "You're worried about screwing things up for me?"

"Of course. This is important to you. I don't want to ruin it by accident."

"Penta." He said her name with an air of helpless confusion.

Great. She'd already made him uncomfortable. She opened her mouth to apologize, but the words froze in her throat when his hands rested on her shoulders and his lips covered hers.

Chapter Eight

Penta's full, rich flavour flooded Cash's senses. Suppressing the desire to dip his tongue into the wet warmth of her mouth, he kept the kiss light and delicate. The gap between their bodies seemed a terrible waste of space. He wanted to press her softness against him, grip her lush ass with both hands. Instead, he kept his fingers on the roundness of her shoulders covered by the cotton of her enveloping sweatshirt.

He was increasingly curious to see what was underneath her shapeless clothing.

Some idiot gunned a motor on the street. He lifted his head and let his hands slide down her biceps before dropping to his sides.

She blinked, speechless, her obvious befuddlement a satisfactory surprise.

"Umm." She licked her lips. His gaze zeroed in on their shiny pinkness. "What was that for?"

"A thank you. For worrying about me and Elle." He couldn't remember the last time someone had put his needs first. "We don't need a safe word, Penta. I'll be honest with you, and you'll be honest with me. The rest will work itself out."

He could actually see her drawing her wits about her. "Sure. If that's what you want."

He was beginning to worry about exactly how much he wanted from Penta. Pressing the latch, he drew the door open. "After you."

She stepped past, a little uncertain on her feet. If that was how she reacted to a simple kiss, what would she be like if he lavished his full attention on her?

The thought came back to him later that night as he lay in his queen-sized bed, arms crossed behind his head and stared at the ceiling. He hardened at the memory of her sweetness, her surprise. His right hand itched to relieve the pressure, but he didn't move. For reasons he couldn't decipher, it would be wrong to jerk off while thinking of Penta.

He couldn't remember much of the hour or so he'd spent with the Silverberries. It had been pleasant enough and he hadn't felt as out of place as he usually did.

He *could* remember every nuance of the brief kiss he'd given Penta.

And wondered if she'd mind if he did it again—did it *right*—someday.

The next afternoon, Penta parked in front of Absolute Motorcycle Repair just as a large service van pulled away. The disfiguring plywood that had hid the destruction Cyril and his friends had wrought was gone. In its place, glossy, pristine glass gave passersby an unimpeded view of the space inside.

Through the wide window nearest her, she observed Cash talking with a blond girl wearing the teenager's ubiquitous uniform of backpack slung over one shoulder, T-shirt, and tight jeans encasing sturdy legs. Cyril straightened products on a nearby shelf, head half-turned, as if eavesdropping on the conversation.

The girl gestured as she spoke, hands waving with abandon. Cash regarded her with a blank expression, but something in his stance reminded Penta of a dam on the verge of bursting.

She'd eat her hat if that wasn't Elle.

Taking a deep breath, she left the safety of her van

and entered the shop. The air was thick with tension, and she caught the tail end of the girl's speech.

"It's my birthday, Dad. I don't care what Mom says."

Cash caught Penta's eye, a wild and desperate plea flickering in his grey gaze. She'd hoped they'd have time to strategize how to tell their families about their so-called relationship, but it looked like she'd have to wing it. The current situation needed to be defused quickly, given Elle's shiny eyes and trembling lips.

"Hello, there." She took a position by Cash's elbow, not touching but close enough to present a united front. If anything, the girl's expression grew stormier. "You must be Elle. Cash has told me a lot about you." *A lot* was stretching it. She'd have to get him to rectify that omission soon.

The teenager's gaze flashed from her father to Penta and back again. "He has?"

It was impossible to miss the hopefulness leaching through the surly tone. She nodded, smiling cheerfully. "I'm Penta." She pointed in her son's direction. "Cyril's mother."

"So?"

Someone not familiar with teens might take the dismissive tone as an insult. She knew from personal experience, however, that any response was better than none. "He's how I met your dad."

Her son shot her a glance that held a mixture of dismay and alarm. Was he worried she'd out him as a delinquent? He drifted over, dust cloth drooping from his hand, trying to hide his curiosity behind shuttered eyelids and pinched lips.

Cash said nothing. His chest rose and fell in long, intentional breaths as if he was struggling for calm.

Vividly aware of his burning gaze, and hoping she was doing the right thing, she addressed Cyril. "I was going to tell everyone at dinner tonight, but I guess you'll be the first to know. Cash and I are dating."

Both teens stared, open-mouthed.

Elle recovered a fraction faster. "You are?"

Cyril's words tangled with hers. "Does Dad know?"

"Yes to Elle, no to you." She wasn't looking forward to telling Mark, but Cash would wonder if she didn't. "I wanted to tell you kids first."

Elle regarded her with deep suspicion. The poor girl had just found her father and was probably thinking she'd have to compete with Penta for his attention. She hurried to soothe her. "Cash told me that your mom's a little worried about letting you spend time together. We're hoping she might be more comfortable if I'm around."

"What, like a chaperone?" Disgust dripped from each word. "He's my *dad*. We don't need a babysitter."

"It's a compromise. What would you prefer— fighting with your mom every time you want to see your dad, or having me around to smooth the way?"

Cash could have kissed Penta. And, again, it wouldn't be from lust but gratitude.

Elle had shown up fifteen minutes ago. It was the first time since her original unexpected appearance and his heart had leaped. Maybe Linda had softened her stance, had allowed Elle to come.

No. His daughter had once again slipped her leash and shown up without her mother's approval.

She'd invited him to help celebrate her birthday. "It's not really until Thursday," she'd explained shyly, not knowing the date was engraved on his soul. "But we're having the party Saturday since that's a school night."

He'd tried to explain that he couldn't, that her mother wouldn't allow it. His daughter hadn't accepted his excuses.

Because that's what they were. Penta had agreed to pretend to be his girlfriend for exactly this sort of situation. Yet he hadn't told Elle about her.

The reason he'd said nothing was currently

regarding him with a suspicious eye. Cyril's behaviour this morning had given Cash no hint if Penta had mentioned him to her family yet. No way in hell was he blurting it out.

Watching her now, fielding almost-rude comments from both their children with aplomb, pride mixed with relief swelled in his chest. She knew how to handle teenage angst and drama. Thank god. Because he didn't have a clue.

It was time he got it in gear, though. Penta had broken the ice and settled things down. Now it was his turn to do the adulting.

"What about this?" Three heads swivelled toward him. His brows tightened in a frown, which he immediately relaxed. "I'll talk with your mom. She doesn't know about Penta yet. If she agrees, we'll come to your party."

Elle's face lit up like a neon sign, incandescent with happiness. He hurried to tamp down her enthusiasm. "I'm not promising anything. It's up to your mom. But if she doesn't want me at the party, I'll try and convince her to let us spend some time together soon. An afternoon at a lake, maybe. Or dinner out."

"Awesome!" She sprang forward, her cheek pressed against his breastbone, arms encircling his waist. With cautious awe, he embraced her, impeded by the backpack hanging off her shoulder, but not caring an iota.

For the first time in his life, he was holding his baby girl. He squeezed his eyes shut, trapping tears of joy and regret, and tried to memorize every sensation in case it never happened again.

Far too soon she released him, brushing her hands down her shirt front, eyes sparkling. "When will you call her? Now?"

His arms achingly empty, his heart bruisingly full, he didn't reply right away. He would need to repair his emotional armour before taking on Linda. Elle's excitement sputtered like a blocked carburetor. It tore his heart, and he ground out his answer. "Tonight. I'll call her tonight."

"Awesome," Elle repeated. A chime sounded from somewhere on her person. "That's my alarm. I have to go. The bus will be at the stop soon." She walked backward toward the door as if unwilling to take her eyes off him. "You'll call her tonight? You promise?"

He nodded, the stone in his gut growing harder and colder. Linda would be furious at this turn of events. He could only hope she'd calm down enough to listen.

Events were moving so quickly Penta was dizzy. She'd expected to have a few days to get used to the idea of fake-dating Cash before revealing it to the world. Instead, they'd been dumped into it willy-nilly.

She didn't even have a chance to discuss details after Elle left. The normally snail-like Cyril vanished into the back, reappeared with his backpack, and slouched out of the shop before she had a chance to do more than smile reassuringly at Cash.

With a helpless shrug, she followed her son, pausing at the brand-new door. Cash looked shell-shocked and she wondered if he felt the same sense of distorted reality she did. "Let me know how the phone call goes?"

He stared at her wordlessly.

"Mom!" Cyril hovered by the van, rattling the handle impatiently. Without looking away from Cash, she unlocked it with her fob.

"I mean it. Call me, whatever time it is." She wouldn't be able to sleep until she knew what had happened. "We have to make plans."

He nodded, the skin of his cheekbones tight and pale above the vibrancy of his beard. She took a step toward him, wanting to offer comfort, reassurance. Anything to take the brittle rigidness from his stance.

Her van horn honked angrily. She spun and narrowed a glare at Cyril. "I'm coming!" She turned back to Cash. "Talk later?"

He nodded again, a sharp short jerk of acknowledgment.

On the way home, she rehearsed what to say to her other children. Cyril remained morose and silent, which gave her no clues on how to approach the topic.

That night over lasagna, she told Felix, Delilah, and Abra about Cash. They knew about the break-in—there'd been no hiding Cyril's forced labour—so she didn't have to explain how she'd met him.

The girls appeared unconcerned by the news. After all, their father had already remarried and given them stepsiblings. Their mother dating was pretty low stress compared to that.

Felix, however, interrogated her throughout the meal. She answered as best she could, keeping closemouthed about Cash's stint in prison. Her oldest son considered himself her protector and she didn't want to prejudice him before they'd met.

She crawled into bed shortly after the kids were settled in their rooms. In order from eldest to youngest, they would be studying, playing a video game, streaming TikTok, and sleeping.

This quiet time was her favourite for reading. Tonight, her attention kept drifting to the phone charging on her bedside table.

It was a few minutes past ten o'clock and her eyes were drooping with fatigue when it finally rang. She snatched it up so roughly the charging cord yanked out.

"Cash? How did it go?"

His voice was raw and scratchy, hoarse with hope. "She said yes. The birthday party is a go."

Chapter Nine

This was a *mistake.*

Cash stood with Penta in an out-of-the-way corner of the noisy crowded room and wished he was anywhere else.

Well, maybe not jail, but anywhere other than that.

After her first delighted welcome, Elle had abandoned him for the numerous family and friends who had come to celebrate her sixteenth birthday. Linda was pretending he wasn't there, while her father watched him with a forbidding expression, pointing a warning finger every time Cash accidentally caught his eye.

As if he could stop Cash from doing anything he wanted. The other man was thirty years older, six inches shorter, and fifty pounds heavier, all of it in his gut.

Cash pulled the brake on his whirling thoughts. If Linda knew he was contemplating a fist fight with her dad, she would kick him out, and he would deserve it. Slimy self-disgust coated his simmering frustration but did nothing to cool it.

"How are you holding up?" Penta's voice was soft with concern, her touch on his arm warm and tender.

He twitched out of her reach. "Fine."

He shouldn't take out his resentment on her. She was acting exactly as he'd hoped—friendly, polite, and open. He kind of hated her for fitting in better than he did.

"I don't think she realized what it would be like when she invited you."

Elle was laughing with two kids a few years younger. He thought they were her cousins—Linda's brother's son and daughter—but since he and Penta hadn't been introduced to anyone, he didn't know for sure.

When they had arrived twenty minutes ago, Elle had dragged him in with a triumphant cry. "Hey, everyone! This is my dad!" She'd regarded him with shiny-eyed awe, and he'd almost staggered under the weight. He couldn't believe he was responsible for the joy in her face.

Then Linda had called her away and he and Penta had become nothing but ghosts, looking in from the outside of the warm family circle.

She continued, her tone thoughtful. "I wonder if that's why Linda agreed to let us come."

He appreciated the *us*. It made him feel less alone. His curiosity piqued by her words, he managed an inquiring grunt.

"What better way to keep you apart while giving in to what Elle wanted? She'll be too busy today to spend time with you."

Before he could decide whether to be appeased or irritated by this, Linda announced it was time for Elle to open her presents and his anxiety kicked into an all-new gear.

Penta had offered to help him choose a gift, but he'd wanted to do it on his own. After ten minutes of wandering around a local department store, he'd realized he'd made a horrible mistake. What did he know about teenage girls? Nothing. What did he know about Elle? Not much more.

He'd almost had a panic attack right then and there. His terror had deepened as he eyed the rack of greeting cards, paralyzed by the dozens of choices, none of which suited the situation. Those for daughters mocked his absence from Elle's life and he refused to buy a funny one. The question of what to write inside twisted his gut. Should he sign it *Love, Dad*? Or was that just weird?

With a sense of certain doom, he'd made his decisions and fled the store, sweaty and breathless.

Elle reached for his gift. Black spots whirled in his vision.

Penta was so furious she wanted to hit something. Her teeth ground together behind the calm, meaningless smile plastered on her face.

She couldn't believe Linda was so cruel as to finally allow Cash to be a part of their daughter's life— and then keep him ostracized and isolated. She hadn't even offered them a drink or invited them to nibble the appetizers and snacks covering the kitchen counter.

This was worse than not coming at all. It only highlighted Cash's estrangement.

Never verbose, he'd grown grimmer and grimmer the longer they stood in their corner. She thought he might have a small reprieve as Elle, sitting cross-legged on the living room carpet, worked her way through colourful gift bags and boxes.

Instead, his tension tightened until she could feel him trembling.

She should have insisted on helping him choose a present. Gift-giving was fraught with tripwires and landmines, especially when a teenage girl was involved. And if that teenage girl was a daughter you'd only just met...

She shuddered. *Please god, let him have picked right.*

Elle plucked a flat, rectangular package from the pile. Penta hadn't thought it possible, but Cash stiffened further. She slid him a worried glance. His profile was tense and rigid, the creases around his mouth deep with strain, and his gaze was locked on the gift in Elle's hands.

This is it, she thought, her own gut coiling and uncoiling like a worm on a hook.

"There's no card on this one." Elle looked expectantly around the room.

"It's from me." Cash's words rumbled like rocks rolling downhill.

Elle's expression lit with heart-aching anticipation. Penta's pulse tripped rapidly, and she prayed with all her might.

Unlike the careless enthusiasm with which she'd torn into the other gifts, the girl peeled off the tape and unfolded the paper with respect.

"Oh." Elle's exclamation was soft and worshipful. She lifted a book bound in smooth tan leather out of the wrappings. Penta could see the gilt edges and a red silk ribbon dangling from the spine. Elle opened it reverently, revealing thick cream pages. "It's a journal."

Cash cleared his throat. "Your mom told me you wrote poetry. Thought you could use it for that."

Penta recalled the day Linda had stormed into Cash's shop. She'd forgotten the brief mention of Elle's writing. Obviously, he hadn't. She wanted to hug him for thinking of such a perfect gift.

Wait a minute. I'm supposed to be his girlfriend. Why shouldn't I?

She slid both arms around his waist and laid her head on his shoulder. After a frozen instant, he tugged her closer. The top two buttons of his crisply ironed, pale green dress shirt were unfastened, revealing a few curling red hairs. Her calf, bare below her knee-length capris, brushed the stiff fabric of his patently new jeans. The care he'd taken with his appearance made her weepy. He wanted his relationship with Elle to work so badly.

"Thank you." Elle stroked the book, hugged it to her chest, and stared at Cash with damp eyes. "Thank you so much."

"Here's the one from Gramma and Gramps. Open it next." Linda's strident voice broke the connection between father and daughter.

Penta jerked, startled out of the moment. Cash's arm tightened and he looked down with raised eyebrows, as if surprised to see her there. His lashes flickered, hiding the thoughts swirling in the steel-grey depths, and she thought he might release her. When he didn't, she allowed herself to relax.

The heat of his body stretched from her shoulder to knee, sizzling her nerves and fizzing in her veins. She shouldn't enjoy his embrace so much, but it had been a long time since a man had held her in any way.

She'd let herself revel in it. Just for a few minutes.

Giddy with the success of his gift, Cash almost enjoyed the next hour of the party. He sang "Happy Birthday" unashamedly off key and clapped when Elle blew out the candles.

Penta's presence enhanced his unfamiliar sense of well-being. She never left his side, touching him often and watching the crowd with suspicion, as if guarding him from attack. He felt like an elephant being protected by a mouse. The thought made him grin. His cheeks ached, muscles unaccustomed to smiling weary from overuse.

The day would have ended on a high note if only they'd left right after the cake had been served. But he was greedy, not wanting to miss a moment. After all, he had sixteen years of birthday parties to make up for.

He barely took his eyes off Elle, drinking in every tilt of her head, every glittering smile, every carefree laugh. Which was why he saw her check her phone, cast a wary look at her mother who was busy in the kitchen, and then sidle out of the living room.

"Do you know where the bathroom is?"

Puzzling over Elle's furtive behaviour, he answered Penta absently. "Down the hall on the left, I think."

She nodded and bustled away, leaving him alone for the first time all afternoon.

A couple minutes later, when Elle still hadn't returned, he left the living room the same way she had and found himself in a hall leading to the back door. He headed to the exit and opened it.

Linda and Elle lived in a neighbourhood on the opposite side of town from Penta. It was older with smaller homes and larger yards, but neat and tidy and a far cry from the tumbledown, decrepit buildings where Cash had grown up. He couldn't fault Linda for how she'd raised their daughter. It was clear she worked hard to give her a good life. Probably a better life than if he'd been in it.

The thought made him grateful and angry in equal proportions.

Elle was nowhere in sight. As he turned to go back inside, he spotted movement in the shadows darkening the narrow strip of beaten earth between the house and the fence that separated it from the neighbour.

Elle, squirming in the arms of a youth wearing baggy jeans, a ratty sweatshirt, and a backward ball cap.

Cash reached them in three long rapid strides. Gripping the boy by the back of the neck, he yanked him off Elle. She let out a shriek. With a wordless growl, he threw the youth against the fence. It creaked and shuddered. The boy slumped in a sprawled heap at its base.

"What are you doing?" Elle's high-pitched cry reached Cash through the red thunder roaring in his ears. Her fists pounded his back as he loomed over the fallen boy. "What are you doing?"

"He was..." He struggled to find words, any words. Fury rampaged through him, and he trembled with the compulsion to lift the youth and throw him again. "He was attacking you. You were trying to get away."

"He wasn't. *I* wasn't! He was *kissing* me." Elle's cheeks were scarlet, tears glistening on the rosy skin. She pushed Cash aside. He let her. Dropping to her knees beside the boy, now groaning and struggling to a sitting position, she glared up. "He's my boyfriend and he was kissing me and you *threw* him! I hate you! I hate you!"

Chapter Ten

Penta was washing up in the bathroom when she heard a roaring shout, followed by high-pitched screeches and feet stomping down the hall. Hands still slippery with soap, she struggled to unlock and open the door and then joined the stream of people racing to the back yard.

Popping up and down on her toes in order to see over the assorted guests and family, she caught glimpses of Cash, fists clenched and shoulders braced, standing near two much smaller figures. Elle crouched beside a boy about Cyril's age sitting on the ground, rubbing his head.

"You've ruined everything!" Elle rose to her feet and shoved Cash in the chest. He took a step back, his face bleak and cold.

"What the hell is going on?" Linda joined the fray, ranging herself beside Elle and regarding Cash with an expression on which smug satisfaction and honest concern battled. "What did you do, Cash?"

"I'm sorry." He spoke quietly. The crowd, expressions exhibiting both fascination and horror, barely breathed. "I thought she was in trouble."

"He threw Aaron against the fence." Elle knelt beside the boy again, her words stuttering out between sobs. "Are you hurt? Did he hurt you?"

"I'm fine." The boy shrugged off the hand she placed on his shoulder, ears and cheeks cherry bright.

"He was kissing her. She was struggling." Cash's

monotone sent fear trickling down Penta's spine. He sounded so...lost. So broken.

"I wasn't struggling. We were *kissing*." Elle's voice cracked. "I'm sorry, Aaron. Please don't dump me because of *him*. Please."

Linda lifted her chin at Cash. "I think you should go."

Without a word, he twisted on his heels and vanished in the direction of the street.

Penta dashed into the house, down the hall, and out the front door, snatching up her purse on the way. Cash had brought her to the party, and in his current state he might forget all about her. Not that she would blame him. She couldn't imagine how he was feeling.

She had the sneaking suspicion he had overreacted to seeing his daughter being embraced. But the boy appeared unhurt, only embarrassed. Cash needed to know that she, if no one else, was willing to listen to his side of the story.

His dark blue pickup was parked a few houses away. The rear lights flashed as the engine started and she scurried down the street, panting from her unaccustomed sprint. Reaching the driver's side door, she knocked on the window to catch his attention.

His head turned slowly, as if his muscles weren't under his control. Though he appeared to meet her eyes, she wasn't sure he was seeing anything other than the disaster he'd left behind.

"Stay right there." Not waiting for a reply, she hustled around the hood, scrambled into the cab, and sank onto the seat.

Her command to remain parked didn't appear to have been necessary. Though the truck was running, he made no move toward the gear shift.

After several moments of silence, during which she struggled to find something to say that wouldn't sound condemning or condescending, Cash spoke.

"Are you sure you want to be seen with me?" His tone was so bitter she was surprised frost didn't appear on the windshield. "I'm the guy that attacks children, after all."

"I'll grant you may have been a bit rough and probably terrified the kid, but you didn't hurt him." The urge to shield him—from himself, if necessary— was almost as strong as the familiar urge to shield her children when they did stupid things. "You were protecting Elle."

Despair leeched from every cell in his body. "From her boyfriend. I'm a fool. Elle is never going to talk to me again."

She wouldn't give him false hope. "You haven't helped matters at all, no. But are you going to give up after one mistake?"

His glance was heavy with shame. "It was a pretty big mistake."

"Wait until things calm down and then reach out to Elle. Apologize, grovel, do whatever it takes to fix it." She huffed a short laugh. "If anyone had told me how many mistakes I'd make as a parent, I would never have believed them. But children are resilient, both in mind and body. Elle *wants* to love you. She'll forgive you." Then, because she had to be honest, added, "In the end."

His beard twitched as the corner of his mouth quirked. "In the end." Some of the tension eased from his shoulders. "I imagine you won't want Cyril near me after seeing that. He doesn't have to come anymore. And if you want out of *our* agreement"—he wriggled his shoulders in a rolling motion that revealed his internal discomfort more than any words could— "I'll understand. I don't think you signed on for this."

"Maybe not, but I don't want out. And Cyril owes you every hour. If you were going to be a danger to him, it would have been the night you caught him, not now." Cash's hand clenched on his thigh, the bones stark and white beneath the skin. Giving into impulse, she reached out and squirmed her fingers into his tight fist. He resisted a moment before intertwining their hands, holding on so hard her knuckles ground together. She didn't protest and in a moment his grip eased. "I don't want to be all gushy and sentimental, but you're my friend, Cash. I'm not giving up on you. And I won't let you give up on yourself."

Cash couldn't understand Penta. He'd used brute force against a teenager, for fuck's sake. She should be going all Momma Bear and threatening retribution if he went near her or her kids ever again.

Yet, here she was, declaring that he was her friend. And holding his hand. He'd never imagined how such a simple connection could be so affirming, so consoling.

So arousing.

How inappropriate could his body be? His stones should be shrivelled from humiliation, not drawing up tight with desire. He scolded his stiffening cock into submission.

Squeezing her hand gently in a gesture he hoped she'd interpret as thanks, he released her, put the truck in gear, and rolled out onto the street.

A few minutes later, he parked at the curb in front of Penta's house. Cyril and a young man who looked enough like him to assume he was Penta's other son were playing one-on-one in the driveway, shooting a worn basketball into a freestanding hoop with a tattered net. The older youth snatched the ball from Cyril's grip and then stood still, tossing it back and forth between his hands while staring at Cash, eyes narrowed.

Penta made no move to escape the cab. "That's Felix. My eldest."

"I don't think he likes me." He could respect the boy's instincts, even as he wished for a different response.

"Don't take it personally." She scrubbed her palms

on her thighs. "He's been protective of me since his dad and I split up."

On the driveway, Cyril batted the ball away from his brother and the game resumed, though Felix managed to throw wary glances in Cash's direction with disturbing frequency.

"Want to come and meet them and the girls? They should be home too."

He could read nothing but calm welcome in Penta's question. Twisting slightly in his seat, he faced her. "You really mean to go on with this? After everything that just happened?"

Her nose wrinkled as she pressed her lips together before answering. "I do. You haven't done anything to help my street cred yet."

He didn't laugh at her use of the ridiculous phrase this time but appreciated her attempt to lighten the mood. "If you're sure..."

"I am." She opened the door and shot a challenging look over her shoulder. "Coming?"

Oh, what the hell. "The day can't get much worse, I suppose."

Penta laughed. "You obviously haven't spent much time around kids. It can *always* get worse." Her eyes glinted and sparkled. "But don't worry, I'll protect you."

Running the gauntlet of Penta's children was a surreal experience. He did his best to focus on the introductions but kept flashing back to the instant he'd taken a grip on Aaron's oily scruff and yanked him away from Elle. When would he learn to ask questions before reacting with violence?

Cyril, of course, had no reaction to his presence. Felix continued to regard him with deep suspicion, which actually reassured Cash. At least Penta had someone looking out for her. Delilah reminded him of Elle, not in looks but in age and attitude, and brought home what he'd lost today with such force he couldn't breathe for several heartbeats.

Penta tracked down her youngest in her bedroom. He stepped in gingerly, overwhelmed by the pink frilliness. Pink walls, pink bedspread, pink curtains. Stuffed animals stared beadily at him from a haphazard pile in the corner.

"Abra, I'd like you to meet Cash."

"Hi." The girl sat cross-legged on the floor, surrounded by a mosaic of colourful paper, photos, and glitter-covered shapes. She was a tiny version of Penta with the same curly dark hair, snub nose, and rounded cheeks.

He suddenly felt three times his size, as if his feet were snowshoes, his hands baseball gloves. "Nice to meet you."

"What do you think of this one?" She plucked a piece of paper from the pile around her and held it up. A photo of a sad-eyed puppy with long, floppy brown ears was framed by purple sequins.

"Uh." He glanced at Penta who grinned back unhelpfully. "He's cute?" He couldn't help the questioning lilt.

Abra nodded with satisfaction. "I think so too. He's going on the wall." She waved a small hand at the empty strings pinned in a long zigzag pattern that started about two feet off the floor and reached almost to the ceiling. Tilting her head in a motion that reminded him even more of Penta, she regarded him seriously. "You're taller than Felix. Can you help me put it up?"

Which was how he ended up spending the next half hour decorating an eleven-year-old girl's room. The tiny tyrant knew exactly what she wanted, so thankfully all he had to do was follow orders.

When she finally released him, he staggered down the stairs and found Penta in the kitchen. She looked up from tossing a salad. "Survived, did you?"

"Barely." He'd been distracted from his own woes, but now they returned. "I should be going."

"Do you want to stay for dinner?"

He shook his head. "Thanks, though." He was so used to being alone that a day spent peopling would have been emotionally draining even without the drama at Elle's birthday.

"I understand."

Oddly enough, he believed she did. It was an unexpected comfort.

He was at his truck when he heard her calling. She pattered down the front path, waving a blue envelope in her hand.

"I almost forgot to give this to you."

He took it and read his name in neat cursive on the front. "What is it?"

"Nothing much. But I saw it and thought of you." The tip of her nose pinked, and she couldn't quite meet his eyes. "Don't open it until tomorrow."

Mystified, he nodded.

She rested a hand on his arm and lifted up on her toes. He instinctively dipped his head, and she brushed her lips against his cheek, just above the edge of his beard. "Don't worry. It'll be okay with Elle. Just give her time."

Chapter Eleven

The Sunday after Elle's birthday party was Father's Day. Penta took her children to visit her dad in the morning so they could have brunch with their grandfather. Afterward, Felix drove his siblings to Mark's to spend the rest of the day there.

Which meant she had the whole afternoon to herself.

If she were a good daughter, she'd go back to her dad's to keep him company. Her mother had been gone for just over a year now and, while he seemed to have recovered from the worst of his grief, she knew he was lonely. Since she visited him nearly every day and would go back tomorrow to do his laundry and some light housekeeping, she decided to find a sunny spot in the back yard and relax with a book and a small glass of wine.

She did just that but was unable to settle. The chores four nearly grown children generated were never ending. Reading in the afternoon seemed like playing hooky. Also, she was worried about Cash. He'd had a stressful day yesterday and she knew how accusing the voices in your head could be.

She gave up the battle. Maybe her conscience would let her rest after she'd cleared the kitchen and thrown in a load of laundry.

As she returned from the basement with the boys' hampers, the doorbell rang. Abandoning the dirty linen in the laundry room, she went to open it. If it was a bottle drive, she'd have to say no. She hated disappointing anyone, but Delilah's soccer team had first claim to that revenue.

It wasn't a bottle drive.

It was Cash.

He stood with his toes touching the threshold, so close that his body blocked her view of the driveway. A black leather jacket hugged his broad shoulders, and a helmet hid his bright copper hair. He'd tipped the visor up, revealing gunmetal eyes.

"You gave me a Father's Day card." He unzipped his jacket, reached inside, and pulled out the blue envelope she'd given him yesterday. "A *Father's Day card*. After how I acted."

He sounded baffled and bemused and his head swayed from side to side like a bull expecting an attack.

"I bought it before then." She winced. "What I mean is, you're a father, no matter what. I was looking for one for the kids to give to Mark and thought I'd get one for you too."

"I've never been given one."

She'd assumed as much. Not that she blamed Elle—the girl had no idea who her father was until recently. She could blame Linda, though. It was hard not to judge the other woman when she saw how much Cash wanted a relationship with his daughter. It was important to remind herself that she only knew one side of the story.

Also, she suspected Cash hadn't tried too hard to change her mind. He wasn't exactly a shrinking violet. If he'd wanted to know Elle sooner, he could have forced the issue.

So why hadn't he?

The rattle of a lawnmower starting reminded her they were still standing in the doorway. She stepped back. "Did you want to come in for a drink?"

"I have a different idea." He tucked the envelope back inside his jacket, patting it as if ensuring it was safe. "Do you want to come for a ride?"

Cash had ignored Penta's instructions to wait to open the envelope and was so glad he had. It had taken him almost twenty-four hours to recuperate from the shock. Truth be told, he still wasn't quite recovered.

She'd given him a *Father's Day card.*

It was generic enough. On the front, an artistic rendering of a mountain landscape with a winding road twisting between tall trees was the background for the words *To a Special Man.* Inside, *Happy Father's Day* was printed in plain text.

It was what Penta had written that made his heart squeeze painfully. He'd read it over and over, all evening long.

> *Cash,*
>
> *Being a parent is hard. It's impossible to understand how hard until you are one. Elle might be sixteen years old, but your relationship is like a newborn – fragile yet strong, untested yet indestructible. You're going to make mistakes, and she's going to break your heart in ways you can't even imagine.*
>
> *But it's worth it. My children make me a better person. I wish the same for you.*
>
> *Penta*

For once, he'd been thankful to be alone. His tears had flowed, dripping into his beard, the taste of salt burning his mouth.

The last time he had cried was almost exactly

sixteen years ago. Five months into his three-year sentence, a guard had come to the door of his cell.

"Got a message for you. It's a girl." He clomped away before Cash could catch his breath. Which had been for the best, because letting anyone in prison see you cry was a very bad thing.

Now he stood in Penta's doorway, yearning to repay her belief in him. If she really wanted to be a bad girl—though he was certain her idea of bad was pretty tame—he would take her for a walk on the wild side. Well, wild-ish.

No way was he putting Penta in danger. Ever.

"I brought my spare helmet." He jerked a thumb toward his bike, parked in the driveway. "I figured your kids would be with their dad, so was hoping you'd have time for a ride."

"Where would we go?" She nibbled her lower lip, head canted to one side in the way she did when she was thinking hard.

"Wherever the bike takes us." He had a destination in mind, but figured the mystery would play into Penta's need to step out of her ordinary.

She looked over her shoulder, indecision clouding her face. "I was just putting in a load of laundry."

"Would a bad girl do laundry instead of going for a ride with her tattooed ex-con of a fake boyfriend?"

She squared her shoulders. "No, she wouldn't. Let's do it. The kids won't be back until around eight."

He held back a chuckle. Her determination to break the rules while still being a responsible mother was adorable.

Good god. When had he started even *thinking* words like adorable?

"Should I change?"

Elle's birthday party was the first time he'd seen Penta in anything other than loose pants and oversized hoodies. He wouldn't be a guy if he hadn't appreciated how the tighter fit of her new-to-him look highlighted the curves of her body in delectable ways.

Today she was back to her usual wardrobe.

He cleared his throat. "You might want to put on a jacket. It will feel cool while we're riding. Something in leather or canvas or heavy denim. Also, the boots you wore for the training course, if you still have them."

"Okay then. I'll be right back." She disappeared toward the kitchen.

A few minutes later, Penta locked the house and joined Cash on the driveway. Her heart pounded in her chest. This wasn't going to be a crawl around a parking lot. But the thought of a Sunday afternoon doing chores in an empty house held no appeal. She wanted *more.*

He nodded with approval at the bomber length canvas coat she'd borrowed from Felix—it was several sizes too big but fit over her sweatshirt—and the heavy boots laced high on her ankles.

"I hope I didn't take too long." She accepted the helmet he held out and placed it on her head. "I couldn't find the jacket right away."

He took the buckle from her fumbling fingers, clicked it under her chin, and efficiently tightened the straps. His knuckles grazed her jaw, and a tremble of awareness swept over her skin.

"You put the load of laundry in, didn't you?"

She smiled guiltily, relieved his expression was indulgent, not annoyed. "It can work while I'm playing."

He laughed, grey eyes glinting as the sun sparked embers off his quivering beard. "I knew you wouldn't be able to leave it." He gave her chin a gentle tap with his fist. "You're a good mom, Penta."

His compliment flustered her almost as much as his touch. "Aw, shucks. You're too kind," she said in an awful attempt at a Southern belle accent.

Then he ruined it. "Even if you do coddle them.

Don't think I didn't notice *you* picked out the Father's Day card for them to give to *their* dad." He slid the visor down over her face.

"I was getting one for my dad anyway. It was just simpler." She tried not to sound defensive but wasn't sure she managed.

He straddled the bike, raised it off the kickstand, swept the prop up, and patted the slightly raised seat behind him. "Hop on. Time to forget being a mom for a while. Time to be Penta Unleashed."

She giggled at that. "Penta Unleashed. Sounds like a bad rock band." Balancing on one foot, she attempted to swing a leg over, but the bike was too tall.

"Use the peg, remember."

"Right. Thanks." *Like getting on a horse.* Once seated behind him, she reached down, searching for the hand grips. "Uh, Cash...?"

He twisted around and she fluttered her fingers near her hips in confusion. His eyebrows waggled wickedly. "Sorry. No grab handles on this one. You'll have to hold onto me."

If she didn't know better, she'd think he was flirting. But that wasn't the arrangement they had. While she could admit to herself she found him more handsome the longer she knew him, she had no illusions about her own ability to attract male attention.

Or inability, as the case may be.

The motor roared into quivering life. "Ready?" He raised his voice over the grumble of the engine.

Oh, god. She hoped she wouldn't embarrass herself. "Ready." She laid her hands lightly on his shoulders. It seemed less intimate than his hips. Even through the layers of clothing she was aware of his heat, his strength.

He pushed with his legs and the bike reversed out of the driveway. In the residential area and as Cash weaved their way out of the city at a modest pace, she kept her balance easily, though she didn't risk taking her hands off him. Once they hit the highway heading east, though, she discarded all notions of propriety and wrapped her arms around his waist, clenched her thighs around his, and clung like a limpet.

"All right?" His shout whipped past her ears.

"Yes." This was what she wanted—to be pushed from her comfort zone. No way was she going to admit her fears.

"Don't worry. I've got you. Just remember to lean *with* me in the corners."

A speed limit sign blurred passed. She could see the bike's dashboard over his shoulder and noticed he was travelling a few kilometres slower than what was posted. She appreciated that he was doing what he could to make her feel safe but hated to dampen his own enjoyment.

"You can go faster if you want." Her helmet bumped his as she spoke near his ear.

"Are you sure?"

"I'm sure. Penta Unleashed, remember?"

His laughter rumbled, vibrating against her chest, and he twisted the throttle.

Chapter Twelve

While they were on the main highway, Cash kept strictly to the speed limit. Once they were on a secondary road that followed the railway line heading east, he gradually increased the speed until Penta wondered if they'd take flight.

She balanced on the razorback divide between terror and elation. Adrenaline flooded her nerves, and her breath panted raggedly from her lungs. A particularly sharp corner had him leaning the monster bike so far over she was sure his knee scraped the road's rough surface. She fought the instinct to remain vertical and leaned with him, helmeted head heavy and unwieldy, eyes closed to avoid the sight of impending death.

When they came out of the corner unscathed and were once more upright, she pried open her eyelids and lifted her chin. An isolated farmhouse flashed by, followed by an undulating ribbon of sagging barbed wire held up by crooked fence posts. A long straight stretch disappeared into the distance, and she braced for speed. Instead, their momentum slowed, and Cash pulled off the road onto a narrow drive barricaded by a metal gate.

Balancing the bike with his feet planted on the gravel, he removed his helmet. Penta realized she was still fastened to him like duct tape and hurriedly retracted her arms and straightened her spine.

He shifted in his seat without disturbing the bike's equilibrium, twisting to look at her. "How are you doing?" His eyes glinted, polished silver in the afternoon sun.

Her fingers trembling with exhilaration, she had only one answer. "I'm alive."

His forehead creased. "You should have told me to slow down."

"That's not what I meant." She scrambled to explain. "I *feel* alive. Not just existing, but alive. The world is brighter and louder and I can *hear* my body. My pulse, my breath, my nerve endings. It's amazing."

His expression lightened. "That's how I feel too."

Though she'd released him from her death grip, her thighs still bracketed his hips and her breasts brushed his back when she inhaled. As if realizing the same thing at the same time, Cash's eyes darkened to pewter. She fell into his starlit stare, connected not just physically but by shared experiences, shared emotions.

Her gaze dropped to his lips, framed by his thick but neatly trimmed beard. For an infinitesimal moment, she considered leaning in for a taste. She'd avoided thinking of the brief kiss he'd given her outside the pub for days now. He hadn't meant anything by it other than thanks, and their fake relationship didn't extend to physical caresses.

With a tiny gasp, she tore her thoughts away from such dangerous pathways. "Is it time to go back, then?" She didn't want their ride to be done, but she also didn't want to wear out her welcome.

"We can if you want." Cash stroked his beard with one gloved hand in a gesture she'd begun to suspect indicated nervousness. "But there's something I'd like to show you. If you want."

She scanned the area. Behind her, a huge field green with new grass stretched emptily to low, rolling foothills, mountains blue in the distance. The road was deserted—they'd only seen two other vehicles since leaving the main highway, both heading the opposite direction—and on the other side of the gate, the lane vanished into a thicket of trees. "What is it?"

He unzipped the chest pocket of his leather jacket and fished out a key ring. "It's through there." He pointed to the metal bars. "Do you trust me?"

Cash's heart thudded heavily, and not just from the sexual tension permeating his body. Yes, having Penta's softness pressed against him, swaying with his, matching the movements of his bike during the ride, had ignited a core-deep glow that hadn't faded. But more than that, he wanted to give her a gift that revealed exactly how much the words she'd written in his first ever Father's Day card meant to him.

If she said yes, he'd be disclosing something very few people knew, sharing a part of himself that was raw and painful even after years of healing.

He very badly wanted her to say yes.

"Of course I trust you." The corners of her eyes wrinkled in a wry expression. "I wouldn't be here if I didn't."

"Good." He pressed a fist against his breastbone in a pathetic attempt to dislodge the sensation wedged there, then replaced his helmet, leaving it unbuckled. "Good. Let me open the gate."

"I'll do it." She plucked the fob from his fingers and wriggled off the seat. He closed his eyes against the onslaught of breast and belly. "Which key is it?"

He pointed it out, breathing deeply to control his inappropriate urges. She deftly opened the padlock and dragged half the gate to the side. After he drove the bike through in first gear, she swung it closed and locked it again. Having her squirm into place behind him was another moment of sweet torture, but she felt right seated on the two-up in ways he didn't want to examine.

The gravel lane was pocked with holes large enough to catch a tire and he steered carefully around them. Penta's weight shifted lightly as she swung her head from side to side.

In less than two minutes, he took the final turn, and the facility came into view. He parked next to the large wood-framed main building and turned off the engine. He hoped she wouldn't be disappointed with his surprise.

"Welcome to Camp Chance," he said.

"Is it a summer camp for kids?" Penta swung her leg over and stepped away from the bike, turning in a circle as she took in the four long, low residences, the army-style obstacle course, the open-walled pavilion with its peeled wood posts and shingle roof.

"Sort of. It's a youth-at-risk centre." He dismounted, hips and back complaining faintly.

"Really?" She unbuckled her helmet and ran her fingers through the strands, fluffing the curls. The colour made him think of coffee grounds sprinkled with salt. "How long has it been here? I've never heard of it."

"About twenty years. We keep a pretty low profile."

She paused in her scrutiny to slide him a glance. "We?"

"I volunteer." And donated money when he had a little extra, which wasn't often. "There are paid staff, of course, and it's run by a well-known society. But the existence of the camp is kept quiet."

"Why?"

"A variety of reasons. Mostly for security and to protect the privacy of the residents."

"I see." A flicker with a red cap and a cream breast speckled with black flew by in a dipping, swooping motion, uttering a sharp *kyeer-kyeer*. "How long have you been a volunteer?"

"About eight years." All staff and volunteers had to pass a criminal record check. He'd had to jump through a few extra hoops to get approved, but the camp counsellors had been eager to have him, seeing his prison stint as an advantage. He was someone who had *been there*, someone who could speak from experience.

"Is anyone here now?" She peered from side to side as if expecting people to magically materialize.

"No. The next intake is tomorrow. All visitors need to have prior clearance."

Her grin flashed as swift and sharp as the flicker that had winged past. "Did you just sneak me into somewhere I'm not allowed?"

Her teasing startled a bark of laughter out of him. "I guess I did. You're really breaking the rules today."

"I guess I am." She tilted her head inquiringly. "Does Linda know about this?"

"No."

"Why not?"

Words he hadn't intended to utter tumbled from his lips. "I don't want her to know. This is between me and the kids here."

"If she did, she might be more receptive to you and Elle spending time together."

No way in hell was he admitting to this caring, sensitive woman that he hadn't trusted himself to be around Elle. The kids at the camp were different. They were scarred in ways he understood—which meant they understood *him*. Bringing a child untouched by fear, by violence, into his orbit was unthinkable. Linda's decree that he keep away from their daughter had almost been a relief.

The older he got, the more he wondered if he'd accepted her decision out of fear. Had taken the coward's way out, not been noble and self-sacrificing.

He would never forget the look of courageous terror on Elle's face the first time he'd seen her. If a sixteen-year-old girl was brave enough to seek out her father, could he be brave enough to deserve her?

Penta's heart overflowed with affection for this difficult man. He had shared a secret with her, one so private he hadn't used it to mend his relationship with his daughter. It made her feel special, singled out—and *needed* in a way she hadn't felt with another adult in a long, long time.

"Thank you for bringing me here. I'm honoured." She bumped her shoulder against his bicep. "I still think you should tell Linda. Despite some evidence to the contrary"—she made sure to keep her tone light, so he knew she was teasing—"you're a good man, Cash."

His only response was a grunt.

It wasn't her place to push it, so she let the moment pass. "Can I have a tour? Is that allowed?"

He unclipped his helmet, took hers from her hand, and stowed them on the bike. "Sure."

She didn't have to feign interest as he showed her around the small facility. Volunteering here fed his soul, and as the tour went on, he grew animated in a way she'd never seen. He had keys to all the buildings, though only showed her one of the residences. "You've seen one, you've seen them all," he explained.

The back of the main building incorporated a large garage with two overhead doors. He unlocked the person door set between them and led her into a mechanic's shop.

"Let me guess." She waved at the tools, the half-built engine on the wooden workbench, the dismantled bike surrounded by parts standing on an ancient tarp. "This is your domain."

He jerked his shoulder in a self-deprecating motion. "It's what I do. Another volunteer takes them canoeing on the lake that's on the other side of the dorms. Another teaches them how to cook. The counsellors do the heavy lifting with group therapy, anger management, that sort of thing."

"It's good to give them options. Exploration gives kids the chance to discover likes and dislikes. They learn that failing isn't an end, just a step along a new path."

She'd been idly prodding the bits and pieces lined up next to the engine on the worktop. Strong rough fingers gripped her chin and tilted her head. Cash regarded her with an expression in which wonder, hunger, and power mixed.

Warmth spread through her, flushing her cheeks. Her breath lodged solidly in her lungs.

"I really want to kiss you." His hoarse voice ruffled her skin like sandpaper.

The desire stoked by the long ride pressed up against him and the vulnerability he'd expressed earlier flared, dazzling her. She licked her lower lip, accidentally brushing his thumb. His pupils, already dilated in the dim light, expanded further and he growled.

He *growled*.

Penta Unleashed, she reminded herself. She licked her lip again, this time deliberately swiping her tongue against his finger. "Why don't you, then?"

Chapter Thirteen

Cash's stormy gaze welded itself to Penta's, his light clasp on her chin tightening. She held herself still, waiting like a mouse in a trap. A willing mouse in a pain-free trap but caught all the same.

"I didn't think that was part of our agreement." The words ground out from between his tightly pressed lips.

"We didn't say it wasn't, either. We never discussed"—she swallowed and then made herself continue—"t-touching. And k-kissing." Damn it. She hadn't meant to stutter. But locked in the intensity of his expression, she was surprised she could form complete sentences at all.

"What we have isn't real. Touching you like *this*"— his fingers left her chin to trace the column of her throat in a fiery line—"shouldn't be allowed."

She knew it wasn't real. Could never be real. Being caressed by the tattooed hand of a hard but handsome man after breaking all sorts of speed limits on a motorbike and sneaking into a youth camp wasn't *real*, not in Penta's world. But she couldn't squash the wish that it was. That adventures with this man could be her reality.

"What if I want you to?" With great care and even greater bravery, she laid her palm flat on his chest. The metal zipper of his jacket was cool and sharp, the leather warm and supple. "It d-doesn't have to m-mean anything." Cash would never take her seriously if she kept stuttering.

"You don't sound too certain. Are you sure you're ready for casual sex?" Grim amusement flickered in his smoky eyes.

All she'd wanted was a kiss. An honest to God, proper kiss. She should have guessed his thoughts would leap to sex. Her courage fled. "Never mind. Forget I said anything." Cheeks hot with humiliation, she attempted to spin on her heels. Before she could do more than twist her shoulders, his hands clamped onto her hips and held her in place.

"I can't forget it. Give me a minute." He fell silent and she waited, staring fixedly at the pull tab on the zipper of his jacket.

Finally, he sighed. "I'm not good at this relationship thing. I just don't want you to do something you might regret later." His hands kneaded her flesh, insistently exploring. "I like that you ask for what you want even when it scares you."

She peeked up, wary. "You do?"

"I do. Let's go back to where this started." His growl had softened to a purr. A dangerous purr, but one that promised dark delights. "I really want to kiss you. Do you want me to, Penta?"

She considered his question carefully, trembling as his thumbs traced circles on her waist, his fingertips pressing the tops of her buttocks. "No."

His caresses stopped immediately, and he put an arm's length gap between them. "I see."

"No," she repeated. "I don't think you do."

She stepped forward. He stepped back. She followed him, stride for stride, until he was pressed up against a workbench.

Penta Unleashed. "I don't want you to kiss me, Cash. *I* want to kiss *you.*"

His mouth, encircled by his luxuriant beard, opened and closed. Satisfaction rolled through her at reducing him to speechlessness.

The seconds ticked by, and she clung tightly to her

daring. "Well?" she prodded.

He found his words, his voice husky and raw. "Go right ahead."

His palms were planted on the workbench behind him, his elbows bent. The toes of her heavy riding boots bumped his as she placed her hands on his shoulders. He sucked in a breath, his ribcage rising sharply. With the laces tight around her ankles and unyielding soles, it was difficult to rise onto tiptoes, but she managed with fair grace. Other than bending his neck so she could reach his mouth, he remained bolted in place.

His beard rasped her chin and the corners of her mouth. His lips, dry and a little chapped, clung to hers as she tasted him. She ran her tongue along the seam, and he welcomed her in. When she invaded his warm wetness, his tongue danced with hers almost shyly.

He opened his legs so she was cradled between them, her core pressed against a heavy, hot bulge, her breasts flattened on his chest. His hands hadn't left their positions on the workbench, and she wriggled, wordlessly inviting him to bring them into play. When he didn't take the hint, she drew back just far enough to issue a command. "Touch me."

He groaned and his palms cupped her ass. She whimpered approvingly, rewarding him with little nips along his full bottom lip.

She'd forgotten how much she liked kissing. Liked the sensations, the tastes, the explorations. Liked the anticipation of what could come next without the pressure to perform.

Her arms wound around his neck and her fingers played with the hairs on his nape. It was almost long enough for a ponytail. She'd never like that look on men, but she might be willing to make an exception for him.

She might be willing to make a lot of exceptions for Cash.

Courage had always been an aphrodisiac for Cash, maybe because he wished he had more of it himself. Penta's emotions were easy to read on her face, and he'd watched, fascinated, as she'd swung from nervousness to anger to determination.

He'd expected her kiss to be tentative. Instead, it was bold and teasing. She savoured him with a thoroughness, a tenderness, that made his knees shake.

The round globes of her ass were heavy and full. She seemed to like it when he squeezed, squirming against him, yet never letting her lips leave his for longer than a breath. His neck ached from bending over, but no way in hell was he going to break this connection, so he hefted her up until her toes left the ground.

She squeaked and drew away. "What are you doing? Put me down." Her protest was undermined by her knees clamping onto his hips, her arms wrapping around his shoulders.

"No." He liked the feel of her, solid and soft. But he wasn't as young as he used to be, and his back gave a warning twinge. Compromising, he turned and sat her on the workbench he'd been leaning against. "Now, where were we?"

But the lustful spell had broken. A blush reddened her cheeks and her lashes, naturally thick and dark, swept down to hide her thoughts. She worried her bottom lip with her teeth in a way that had his stiff cock hardening further, and then dropped her head to his shoulder.

"I hate to admit it, but maybe you were right." Her words were muffled against the leather of his coat.

"About what?" Despite her withdrawal, he took heart from the fact she remained in his embrace. He couldn't stop sweeping his palms up and down her back. She still wore her son's heavy canvas jacket over her sweatshirt. He itched to get below the layers, to see and touch *Penta*. Just Penta, with nothing between them.

"Maybe I'm not ready for casual sex. Just kissing you was..."

He waited, but she remained silent. Curiosity gnawed. Had their kiss made her feel as powerful yet vulnerable as it had made him? Or was she already regretting it? "I'd never pressure you into anything you didn't want. You know that, right?" Given she'd seen him attack a teenage boy, it couldn't hurt to state that outright.

She lifted her head, curls catching on his beard with tiny tugs. "I do."

He hadn't bothered turning on the huge fluorescent fixtures on the ceiling. Only a couple of small bulbs hanging on the wall shed any light in the dim space. Sitting with her back to one of them, he couldn't read her expressive face. Her tone, however, was decisive, and he relaxed. "I can't remember the last time I made out with a pretty girl."

Her teeth gleamed in a quick grin. "I was just thinking how much I like kissing. Sex is good too. But sometimes I just want to fool around with no end goal."

If she thought sex was just *good*, her husband hadn't been doing it right. "I'll fool around with you anytime you want."

She'd regained some of her confidence. Her shoulders straightened and her knees tightened, gripping his hips. "Do we have a deal, then? Making out is included?"

"I'll sign on that dotted line." An odd bubbly sensation filled his chest. Happiness hadn't been a part of his life for a long time. Satisfaction, sure. Even contentment. But true joy? Not so much. He'd grown used to regarding anything like it with dread, knowing he was bound to ruin it somehow.

She wasn't done realigning their relationship. "Does this mean we're...I don't know...friends? I know it was supposed to be fake between us, but it doesn't feel that way. Not anymore."

It was never fake for me. That revelation from his subconscious knocked the wind out of his lungs. He sucked air in through his nostrils. How had he fooled himself for so long? He had been attracted to Penta from the start, but the fact now blazing in neon orange was that he *liked* her too. Worse, he *trusted* her.

He uttered a gruff agreement. "I'm good with friends."

Her smile lit up the gloomy garage. "That's a relief. I'm a very bad actor. If we're real friends, doing this will be so much simpler."

He was glad *she* thought so. Because *he* was certain having Penta in his life would be anything but simple.

Cash took the ride back to town at a slower pace, intensely aware of Penta riding pillion. She was much more relaxed, swaying confidently into the corners, hands resting lightly on his waist. Her chin bumped his shoulder from time to time, her breasts squashed against his back, and her thighs bracketed his. He resisted the compulsion to pull off the highway and find a secluded copse of trees where he could continue what they'd started in the garage.

He rolled up her driveway with regret. When he cut the engine, the whine of an out-of-sight power tool reached his ears. Three houses up, two small children drew with chalk on the driveway, watched over by a woman holding a baby and sitting in a lawn chair. Across the street, a man washed a bright blue SUV, soapy water trickling into the gutter.

It was all very suburban. Very pleasant. And very different from the way Cash had grown up.

Penta swung a leg over and slid off the bike. "Thank you so much for the ride." She unbuckled her helmet and handed it to him.

He twisted to clip it to the hook under the passenger seat. "You're welcome."

"Do you want to come in? The kids won't be home for a couple of hours yet." Her cheeks, already rosy from the whip of wind on their journey, brightened. "That wasn't supposed to sound like a proposition."

He wanted to say yes, very badly. He enjoyed spending time with her, no matter what they were doing. But he hadn't screwed up the afternoon yet and didn't want to tempt fate. "Maybe next time."

"Of course." "Of course." The lines around her eyes relaxed. In relief?

"We're good, right?" He stripped off one riding glove and took her hand. Her chilly fingers curled around his.

"More than good." She bussed his cheek in a quick kiss. "I'm glad we talked things out."

"Me too." He gave a gentle squeeze and let go with reluctance. "Now I think it's time I talked things out with Elle."

Her expression softened. "Don't be too hurt if she doesn't forgive you just yet. But don't give her the chance to walk away, either. Let her know you'll be ready to discuss things whenever she is. Just being there is half the battle as a parent."

"Thanks." He fired up the engine.

She patted his shoulder. "Good luck."

He nodded as he let the bike roll backward down the drive and into the street. He was going to need it.

Chapter Fourteen

Despite the mutual decision to escalate their fake relationship to something more, Penta knew it didn't give her the right to pester Cash about his reconciliation with Elle. She would have to wait until he was ready to share the news. By the time she went to her father's on Monday, she had heard nothing and was itching with curiosity, which she buried under loads of laundry and other household chores.

"Lift your feet, Dad." She ran the vacuum under his raised legs and wondered when she'd become this caricature of a 1950s housewife.

Not that it was really a mystery. It had happened when her mother passed away. In the first weeks after his wife's death, Jeremy Wicken had been inconsolable, lost in a fog of grief. Battling her own sorrow, she succumbed to his need and stepped in—preparing his favourite meals, cleaning the house—even taking over the laundry after she found him standing motionless in front of the machines, regarding them as if they were alien life forms.

He lowered his legs, never shifting his attention from the World War II history book he was reading. After retiring from his role as a high school mathematics teacher, he'd been able to fully indulge his passion for the various military conflicts of the twentieth century.

She used to be interested in topics other than what meal to make for dinner or the best way to get stains out of a soccer jersey. In high school, she'd won the Senior Science Award and received a partial scholarship to the brand-new University of Northern British Columbia. She had dreamed of a career making amazing discoveries that would improve the world. What had happened to that girl?

The answer to that question was easy too. She'd become a mom. And while she might be restless and uncertain about her future, she didn't regret one instant of her past. Her children were her everything.

She continued down the hall toward the bedrooms, accompanied by the vacuum canister and an aura of vague exasperation.

During the divorce discussions, she'd welcomed Mark's child support payments as the least he could do after shattering their family. But negotiating for spousal support had made her skin crawl. Her lawyer hadn't let her refuse the money, so she'd set up a separate bank account and vowed not to touch it. Then she'd dusted off her resume and started searching for work.

Unfortunately, she'd been a stay-at-home mom since Felix had been born. A half-completed Science degree almost twenty years ago didn't qualify her for much and she couldn't bear the thought of working evenings or weekends, stealing precious hours from the time her children were not in school.

In the end, she'd decided they were worth swallowing her pride. The older they grew, though, the more she wondered what she would do when they all left home. Abra was graduating from Grade Seven in a couple of weeks, and her high school years would go by in a blink. Where would Penta be then?

She stored the vacuum cleaner in the closet and went back to the living room. "Dad? Can we talk a minute?"

He closed his book, tucking a finger between the pages to mark his place. "Of course."

She perched on the edge of her mother's

upholstered rocker. The clay coaster Cyril had made in kindergarten still waited for her next cup of tea on the table between the two chairs. Though she'd finally convinced her father to donate his wife's clothes to charity, very little else in the house had changed.

"I was thinking it might be time to get a job." The words felt bizarre in her mouth. She had a job, taking care of her family.

"Good for you." His smile was pleased, proud...and relieved?

She must have read that flicker of expression wrong. "If I do, I'll have less time to help here."

"I'm sure I'll manage. I think getting a job is a great idea. If there's anything I can do, just let me know." He opened his book as if the conversation were over.

A sinking sensation kept her rooted in her seat. "Won't you miss me?"

He closed the book again and slid her a shamefaced glance. "You know I appreciate everything you do, and you are welcome to visit whenever you like. But maybe it's time for a change, for both of us."

"How long have you thought this way?" *How long have you been wishing I would just leave you alone?*

He sighed and answered obliquely. "You always seemed so pleased to help out. I didn't want to hurt your feelings."

Humiliation prickled her cheeks. She'd spent much of the last year looking after him and now he was acting like *he* had been doing *her* the favour. He placed the book on the table and folded his arms across his belly. "I'm grateful for all you've done this past year, I really am. But I'm a grown man. You don't really think I do nothing but sit in this chair and read, do you?"

She kind of did, but she wasn't going to admit it. "I know you go to church most weekends. And I guess I don't buy everything you need."

"No. And that's not a slight on how you care for

me." He laid his hand over hers. She was struck by its thinness, the tendons and veins sharply marked on the back. "I suppose this is partly my fault. I should have had this conversation before now, but I like having you around. You have your own life, though, and I understand if you want to get back to it. Maybe we both needed this time together after your mother passed. But things are settled now, don't you think?" His eyes twinkled with familiar mischief. "I still expect frequent visits, and certainly won't say no to any meals you'd like to share. But don't feel guilty for moving on. That's the last thing your mother or I want."

It was ridiculous to feel rejected. Was it too much to ask that he'd at least *pretend* to be upset?

She kissed his cheek in farewell. Normally, she would utter a breezy "See you tomorrow" as she left.

Today, she just said goodbye.

Cash had run into a serious roadblock in his attempt to apologize to Elle.

He didn't have her phone number and didn't want to show up at the house uninvited, so had sent a carefully worded text to Linda on Sunday evening. After twenty-four hours of resounding silence, he sent another, even more humble and apologetic. Another twenty-four unresponsive hours later, he sat in his one-bedroom apartment above the shop and wondered what he should do next, mouth bitter with failure.

He wanted to hear Penta repeat her assurances that everything would be okay. But he hadn't seen or spoken to her since their ride on Sunday. He'd thought he might have a chance that afternoon, but Felix had picked Cyril up.

Had she changed her mind about being friends? Had his volatile temper once again destroyed something precious? The thoughts burned like battery acid, eating away at what little composure he had left.

Wednesday went by with no word, and when he woke Thursday morning—Elle's birthday—he came to two grim conclusions. Penta was avoiding him, and reconciliation with his daughter wasn't going to happen. Even if Linda had kept his attempts to reach her a secret, Elle had braved her mother's wrath to talk with him twice before. Her absence now must mean she no longer wanted him in her life.

He focused his despair and self-loathing on the Baby Bonnie, which was now stripped down to its frame. A few customers ventured in, breaking his concentration, and he managed to be civil to them. At least, he thought he did. When Cyril arrived for his after-school shift, he directed him to the back room to unpack a shipment of parts and supplies. It seemed safest to keep the boy out of his way.

All he wanted was to be alone. It was better for everyone.

He tinkered on the Triumph for several minutes in solitude before Cyril sauntered into the room holding a box about the size of a carry-on suitcase. "Are you sure these are the right filters? It's just that—"

"Of course they're the right ones. I ordered them, didn't I?" Cash heard the snarl in his voice, but even if he hadn't, Cyril's startled expression would have alerted him.

"Jeez, what got up your ass?" The youth's eyes widened further. "Sorry. I didn't mean... I shouldn't have said that."

At least the kid was learning some respect for his elders. If only Cash deserved it. "Ignore me. I'm in a pissy mood. What were you saying?" Cyril rarely wasted his time with stupid questions, a fact he wished he'd remembered before snapping.

"I was checking everything against the order sheet, like you taught me. These filters are the right size and all, but not the same brand you usually get. I just wanted to make sure."

Cash took a closer look at the box. Sheepishness

made him even surlier, though he tried not to bark. "You're right. They aren't what I asked for. I'll call the parts store later. Don't unpack them."

Cyril nodded and turned to go.

"Hey." The boy hesitated, his back to Cash. "I shouldn't have shouted. Thanks for checking with me." A shrug was his only response, though the skinny shoulders relaxed a little. "Who's picking you up tonight?"

"Mom." He answered the question without curiosity and disappeared into the back.

The news chipped a tiny sliver off Cash's gloom. Maybe all wasn't lost with Penta.

Chapter Fifteen

Penta's conversation with her father rankled for several days. She'd been trying to help, and he'd acted like she was smothering him. Oh, he'd been perfectly polite and hadn't actually used that word, but it was what he'd meant.

Echoes of similar comments made by both Mark and Cash only sharpened the sting. She was a loving, caring person. How could that be a bad thing?

Well, if everyone wanted to be left alone, she could do that. She sent Felix to fetch Cyril from Cash's shop and though she picked up the phone to call her father several times, she always put it back down without dialling. One night she refused to make dinner for the kids. Since the fridge was full of leftovers, they might not have noticed her mutiny. These small acts of rebellion made her restless and twitchy and irritated. She hated it.

What made it worse was that neither Cash nor her father reached out to her. Had the agreement she and Cash forged at the youth camp meant that little? And how could her father dismiss the hours of work she'd done so easily?

Tears burned at the back of her throat if she thought about it too long. But with the forlorn sense of abandonment came a growing resolution to make changes in her life.

She dug into her home computer and excavated her last resume. It was a terribly thin document and the dates on it made her wince. How had twenty years gone by so quickly? Searching internet job sites made her feel prehistoric. She didn't know what some of the titles meant, let alone have any of the mysterious qualifications required.

Gradually, her wounded feelings eased, and her cheerful temperament reasserted itself. In this cooler frame of mind, she realized she'd been punishing Cash for something he hadn't done. He may have told her she was too lenient with her kids, but he'd never accused her of overstepping any of his boundaries. In fact, he'd rather encouraged her to do so. Just thinking about their kisses had her cheeks flaming.

Late Thursday afternoon, she parked outside Absolute Motorcycle Repair with the eagerness mixed with angst of a teenager on a first date. When she opened the door, Cash was crouched on the far side of the ancient bike he'd been working on ever since she'd met him. He finished fiddling with whatever he was staring at and straightened, arching his back before finally looking her way. She thought she saw welcome flash across his features before his expression settled into stern blankness.

"Penta." His tone was gruff and formal. He gripped a screwdriver in one hand like a weapon.

His cool reception dimmed her enthusiasm, and her smile slipped. "Cash. How have you been?"

He shrugged, reminding her of Cyril. Were all men just boys with thicker whiskers? "Fine."

She drifted forward until she stood as close as she could get with the bike between them. Dark shadows pooled under his eyes. "You look tired."

Another shrug.

For Pete's sake. Was she going to have to drag it out of him with pliers? "Did I do something to make you angry?"

"No."

"Is it Elle? Is she still mad at you?"

He tossed the screwdriver onto the workbench

with restrained violence. "I imagine so."

"Imagine so? Haven't you talked to her?"

Face shuttered, he picked up a rag, put it down again, picked up a wrench, and then simply stood, turning it over and over in his hand. "Linda didn't return my messages."

Damn the woman. Penta was getting tired of making excuses. It was all well and good to believe she had valid reasons to shun Cash in the past. But that was different now. *He* was different now.

His cold behaviour was starting to make sense. He wasn't angry at her. He was angry at the world.

"What's your plan?"

A third shrug.

"Right then." He might not know what to do, but she did. "It's time to close up shop anyway. We can drop Cyril off at home before we go."

A comical expression of bewilderment creased his face. "Go where?"

"To talk to Elle, of course."

Penta was not to be denied. Despite their size difference, despite his bone-deep reluctance, despite his vocal protests—thirty minutes later he was sitting in the passenger seat of her van parked outside Linda's house, working up the courage to knock on the door.

"You know it's Elle's birthday today." He stared out the window at the neat and tidy bungalow. "Maybe they went for dinner."

"Then we'll wait." Her soft voice was implacable. "I warned you this wouldn't be easy. But you can't let Elle go without an honest attempt to fix things. And I won't let Linda stop you."

Her fierce support eased the cramped, fist-tight muscle that used to be his heart. "Thanks. I'd want you on my side in a bar fight."

That was the wrong thing to say. He'd been trying

to lighten the mood, but his words only reminded him of the catalyst for the shit-show that was his life. His anxiety ramped up again.

Penta made no comment on his inappropriate statement. She unbuckled her seatbelt. "Come on. I'll go with you."

His pride had been battered enough during the last several days. "No. I have to do this myself." He wouldn't hide behind her, no matter how much he might wish to. Unlatching the door, he placed one foot on the pavement and leaned out.

"Cash."

Her hand on his arm stopped him and he ducked his head back inside the van. She stretched over the console and planted a firm, smacking kiss on his lips. "For luck. Take as long as you need. I'll be right here."

He nodded, unable to form words around the rock in his throat.

In the short walk to the front door, he had time to reconsider his decision to go it alone. Seeing Penta at his side might help convince Linda to let him talk to Elle. After all, that's what their fake-turned-real relationship was for. If he turned back now, though, he might never find the balls to try again.

Standing on the low front stoop, he rapped on the door, sweat springing up between his shoulder blades—and not because of the late-afternoon sun shining on his back.

Footsteps sounded from behind the panel, followed by clicking noises as the locks disengaged. He sucked in a deep breath.

Maybe his luck was finally turning because Elle opened the door. When she saw him, her mouth flattened out of its inquisitive smile though her eyes flashed with uncertain welcome. "Hey, Dad."

His internal organs turned to mush. Every single one of them. She still called him *Dad*.

Surreptitiously he slid the toe of his boot over the threshold. He wouldn't force his way in, but he didn't want her shutting the door before he had a chance to say everything. "I need to apologize." No words would ever express the depth of his regret, but he had to start somewhere.

She gave no indication she'd heard him. "You shouldn't come in. Mom's at work."

It wasn't a direct rejection. In fact, it almost sounded like an invitation. "I don't want to get you in trouble." He pointed at Penta sitting in the van. "Would it be okay if we talk outside? Then you can tell your mom Penta was here too."

Elle tucked her bright, straight hair behind her ear. "I guess." She closed the door and settled on the concrete step, wrapping her arms around her denim-clad knees.

He lowered himself beside her, joints popping. The sun shone directly in his eyes, and he shielded them with his hand. "I know nothing will make up for what I did. But I wanted to tell you how sorry I am."

His daughter spoke in a dry adult tone that squeezed his guts. "That seems a good place to start."

Penta watched father and daughter with contentment. They sat shoulder to shoulder, sunlight glinting off straight gold hair and thick red strands. After a few minutes of earnest speech on Cash's part, Elle relaxed out of her protective posture, stretching her legs out and leaning back on her hands. Cash appeared cramped and uncomfortable, practically squatting on the low stoop, but remained still and focused. Neither looked too long or too often at the other, and though the conversation was imperceptible, she could see it progressing in a slow and halting rhythm.

For the first time, she had the leisure to study them together. She thought Elle might have the same shaped face, though it was hard to tell as Cash's jaw was hidden by his beard. Their cheekbones had a similar subtle slant, their foreheads were wide and smooth, and Elle's build was solid and sturdy, just like her father's.

The sun disappeared behind a cloud and the spotlight on the front step dimmed. As if this were a sign, Cash stood up. Elle climbed to her feet too. He said something and trailed his finger down her cheek. The girl's expression lit with a glow of joy so intense it brought tears to Penta's eyes. She desperately wanted to know what Cash had said but would never ask. It was a secret best kept between father and daughter.

Cash waited until Elle was inside the house and then joined Penta in the van. The springs sank as he lowered himself to the seat and leaned against the headrest with a sigh.

"How are you doing?" She searched his profile, pleased to see the lines of strain around his eyes had softened.

"Better. She listened, at least. I think we might be okay."

"I think you'll be more than okay." She gripped his hand where it lay on his heavy thigh and his fingers squeezed back. "I'm proud of you."

"Thanks." He rolled his head toward her, beard jutting. "I never would have done this without you. I just hope Linda isn't too furious."

"You can't control her reactions. You did the right thing, coming here." She wanted to climb into his lap and ravage him. Who knew watching a man reconnect with his child could be so arousing? Instead, she dropped a quick kiss on his nose. "Now, you're coming home for dinner. You shouldn't be alone. It will only give you time to brood."

His big hand cupped the back of her head and drew her close. "Penta."

She shivered. She'd never heard her name uttered with such longing, such affection, such need.

His kiss was nothing as chaste as the one she'd given him. His mouth claimed hers, demanding and pleasuring. He dragged her half over the console, and she planted both hands on his thigh to keep her balance. Muscles flexed powerfully under the denim, rippling with strength. Molten heat swept over her, pumped by a heart that was falling fast.

No. Even as she moaned under his silken assault, her mind rejected the possibility. She wasn't falling in love with Cash. She couldn't. He might hide a sweet vulnerability under his tattooed exterior, but he wasn't in this for the long haul. Once his relationship with Elle had stabilized, it would be over between them. Penta wasn't the adventurous, courageous person who could hold a man like Cash's attention permanently.

She drew back with reluctance, and he let her go. The skin on his cheekbones burned almost as red as his beard and his eyes were charcoal. Their breaths mingled in short, sharp pants.

"I'll take that as a yes to dinner." She turned the ignition key with trembling fingers.

Chapter Sixteen

Less than a week and a half after his fragile reconciliation with his daughter, Cash was once again feeling out of place in a crowd of people he didn't know well. Unlike Elle's birthday, this time the fault was entirely his.

The previous Sunday, he and Penta had gone for another ride. At her suggestion, they'd headed west and stopped at a café with a view of a long narrow lake rimmed with year-round homes and holiday cabins. As they sipped their coffee, she had invited him to her family's traditional June barbeque. "It's a way to celebrate the end of the school year and kick off summer. Since the divorce it's just been me and the kids, a few of their friends, and my parents. This year I'm thinking of inviting Mark and Jacinta. I don't know whether her boys will come."

"And you want me there?" He ripped a piece off the enormous cinnamon bun they were sharing. The bread was soft and warm and sticky with sweetness. Rather like Penta, he thought.

"I don't care what Mark thinks of me but, given what he said the first time you met, I can't wait to see his face when he realizes we're dating." Her grin had turned shy. "That's what this is, right? Dating? It's been so long since I've done it, I'm not sure."

They had yet to progress beyond searing kisses and above-the-clothes caresses. He didn't think he'd ever had a relationship move so slowly. But he was terrified of ruining whatever was growing between them. Penta was the best thing that had happened to him in a long time. Maybe forever. He could wait for her to be ready before moving to the next level.

"Yes," he had answered. "We are definitely dating. And if you want me at the party, I'll come." Even though the thought made him sweat.

The most nerve-wracking thing so far had been meeting Penta's father.

"Call me Jeremy." Mr. Wicken's grip was strong and firm, brown eyes sharp behind silver-framed glasses. "Why don't you get us a couple beers and we'll have a chat."

Despite the ominous tone of the politely worded command, their "chat" had been devoid of confrontation. Jeremy asked thoughtful questions about Cash's business and shared humorous stories from his years teaching high school math. He wished Mr. Wicken had been one of *his* teachers. Maybe he would have done better than scrape by if he'd had more instructors who exuded the same wit and integrity.

They sat on lawn chairs in the back yard. On the deck, Felix manned the barbeque. Abra and Delilah laughed and chattered with their own friends, sprawled on blankets spread over the soft, springy grass. He hadn't seen Cyril yet.

It was all very suburban and domestic, and totally outside his frame of reference.

Penta popped in and out of the house, carrying loads of food and dishes to the outdoor table. Cash had offered to help, but she'd shooed him away. "Go. Talk with Dad about man things. You can help clear up later."

Her assumption he'd stay to the end of the party eased more of his nervousness. She obviously wasn't worried he'd cause another scene. He'd do his damnedest not to betray her trust.

"What has Penta told you about Mark?" Jeremy

sipped from his long-necked bottle, his gaze on his granddaughters.

Cash stiffened. On the surface, Penta and Jeremy had a close, loving relationship. But how much did a daughter tell her father about her marriage? He answered with caution, determined not to betray her confidences. "She said he was the one who asked for a divorce."

"It sounds very bloodless put that way. It was a terrible time. Penta wanted to try counselling. He completely refused. She never said anything outright, but I gather he blamed her, laid the failure of their marriage on her shoulders. Pah." His exclamation was full of contempt.

While Cash shared the same sentiment, he had no idea how he was expected to respond, so kept quiet.

"She's better off without him, but it took her a long time to see that."

Still confused as to *why* Jeremy was telling him these things, Cash only grunted an acknowledgment. The moisture on the bottle of beer he held was a mixture of condensation and palm sweat.

Jeremy turned his bright gaze on him. "Penta told you we lost her mother last year?"

The abrupt topic change set his head spinning faster. "Yes."

"I loved that woman dearly, but she could drive me insane. And I did the same to her. But we trusted each other to never give up. We were a team. That's what I want Penta to have."

A yellow caution flag waved violently in his mind's eye. *Here it comes.*

"If you're going to be like her ex and throw in the towel when the going gets tough, you might as well leave right now." He pointed a finger past Cash, toward the gate leading out of the yard. "And speak of the devil..."

Cash looked over his shoulder to see an obnoxiously grinning Mark stroll in, one arm slung possessively around a tiny dark-haired woman.

Penta stole quick sideways glances at her father and Cash as she ferried food, drink, and other items from the kitchen to the back yard.

In the years since her divorce, she hadn't introduced her dad to any new men—mostly because there had been none. Telling him about Cash would have been fraught with awkwardness even if he hadn't had a prison sentence. Knowing her father's predilection for research, however, she'd made a clean breast of things and braced for a polite but penetrating interrogation.

He'd regarded her speculatively for a second or two and then nodded. "I look forward to meeting him."

And that had been that. It was mystifying. She'd concluded that Jeremy was saving all his questions for Cash.

On her last trip outside, she'd seen nothing worrying—which was in itself a worry. Telling herself not to be silly, she shook off her unease and went to the top of the stairs leading to the basement. "Cyril! It's time to go outside. You can't stay in your room all afternoon."

She heard no reply, but the thumping bass she recognized as the soundtrack from his favourite video game cut off a moment later. Not waiting for him to appear, she picked up a tray loaded with spinach dip, chunks of sourdough bread, and snack crackers, and stepped back onto the deck, just as Mark and Jacinta entered through the side gate.

Her gaze flew to Cash. He was twisted in his seat, watching them arrive. Her father was studying Cash with a teacher-ish expression—one that reminded her of when he'd set an especially tricky problem, but still had high hopes his student would succeed in solving it.

She had no time to deal with that. Placing the tray on the table, she wiped her hands on her hips and went to greet Mark and his new wife.

Keeping her smile firmly fixed on her lips, she let her gaze sweep over Mark to Jacinta. If she'd been the catalyst to their divorce, Penta wasn't sure she could bear to be polite. But Mark had met her a few months after their separation. While her existence stung for many reasons, it didn't have the bitterness of betrayal. "Hello, Jacinta. Thanks for coming."

The other woman nodded, her own smile frank and open. "Thanks so much for including us. Mark tells me he hasn't been invited for a few years."

Oh, no, you don't. You don't get to make me feel guilty about that. Keeping her expression guileless and her tone sugary sweet, she asked, "Your boys didn't come with you?"

"No. They're away at a baseball tournament with their dad."

It had been a bitter pill to swallow when Mark had announced he was remarrying. But it was made a thousand times worse by the fact he was replacing Penta with a woman who had so much in common with her. It underscored his rejection of her as a woman, as a person. Not their life together or their family situation. *Her.*

A heavy arm draped over her shoulders. "Mark." Cash's deep voice rumbled above her head. "Good to see you again."

She wasn't quite sure how, but his tone managed to imply exactly the opposite. A little of the sick tension twisting in her gut eased. *This is why you invited Mark, remember? To show him you've moved on. And with who.*

Mark frowned uncertainly. "I didn't expect you to be here."

"I don't know why not." This time, he managed to imply Mark was dimwitted. Penta's consternation morphed into affectionate amusement at Cash's barely veiled barbs. He dropped a kiss on the crown of her head and pulled her tighter to his side. She leaned in, willing to let him take the lead.

"You're dating?" Her ex narrowed a petulant look at her. "Why didn't you tell me?"

She shrugged, Cash's arm warm and protective, giving her the courage to take her own subtle stab. "Why would you care?"

"Of course I care." Jacinta glared at Mark. He didn't notice.

"You shouldn't." Cash seemed to swell, looming over her softer, squishier ex-husband. "Who Penta dates is none of your business."

Mark didn't back down. "Considering you'll be spending time with my kids, I think it *is*."

As sometimes happens in a group, a sudden silence fell. Before she could offer calming platitudes, Cash's response rang out.

"Are you suggesting Penta would ever put her children in jeopardy?" Menace swirled around him, black and heavy.

Even the birds stopped twittering. Everyone waited for Mark's reply.

"No, of course not." Defeat softened Mark's pugnacious stance.

Penta let out a soft whoosh. The odd moment of frozen time ended, and the world restarted.

"How about a drink?" she said to no one in particular.

Cash made sure Penta's asshole of an ex was occupied before giving in to her insistent tugging. She towed him in the opposite direction, turning to face him when they reached a corner of the yard just out of earshot of the crowd.

He jumped in before she could speak. "I wasn't trying to pick a fight. I just don't like the way that guy treats you."

"I know you weren't. And I could tell." Her eyes creased with devilish amusement as she placed her palms on his bare forearms, her hands soft and warm. "I'm not mad at you. Quite the opposite, in fact."

"You're happy?" That didn't make sense. He'd almost caused a scene. Again.

"Well, pleased. Thanks for sticking up for me, even though I didn't need it." She licked her lips, her gaze dropping to focus on his chest. "Will you stay and help clean up after the party?"

He frowned. "I thought that was the plan."

"And after"—she licked her lips again and a flush rose on her throat— "after that's done, will you take me back to your place?"

He froze, anchored to the earth as if fused by a bolt of lightning. "Come again?"

"I want to be with you, Cash. Tonight."

Chapter Seventeen

After that cock-stiffening statement, the evening couldn't go fast enough. Cash avoided Mark entirely and behaved with formal politeness to everyone else. While Penta seemed to enjoy how he'd tossed Mark's rude words back in his face, he wouldn't give her a reason to change her mind.

Mark and Jacinta left shortly after dinner, but the rest of the guests ignored Cash's subtle glares and seemed determined to stay forever. When—finally!—only he and the family were left, the back yard and kitchen were soon put to rights. Cash gripped his hands behind his back, arousal and need drumming through his veins, and waited with grim patience.

"I'll be off then." Jeremy ruffled Cyril's hair, patted Felix on the shoulder, and gave his daughter and granddaughters hugs. Approaching Cash, he studied him for a moment, and then held out his hand. "It was good to meet you. I hope to see you again soon."

Stunned by this public show of support, Cash shook the other man's hand with gentle firmness. After a final wave, Jeremy said goodbye and disappeared out the door.

The kids scattered, but Penta called them back. "Wait." Cash's nerves snapped like a too tight clutch cable and his breath grew short.

With expressions ranging from curious to bored to annoyed to sleepy, they turned back.

"I'm going to Cash's for a bit." She reached out and

took his hand. Her fingers trembled and he realized anew what a huge step this was. Not just for her. For himself as well. "I'll be back by midnight."

He hadn't expected her to stay until morning, yet he was disappointed. The thought of waking up with Penta beside him was intensely alluring.

Four sets of eyes swung toward him. Even Abra was old enough to understand there was something different going on. He braced in defense.

After a quiet moment, Cyril simply shrugged and trekked down to the basement. Abra hugged her mother and headed in the opposite direction.

Delilah and Felix ranged themselves opposite Penta and Cash.

"Are you going to have sex?" Delilah blurted.

The tips of his ears flamed with heat.

"That's none of your business." Penta's voice was calm, but her fingers clenched his tightly. "If we do, you can be sure we'll be responsible, just like I taught you."

Of course Penta had talked with her children about sex. For all her protectiveness, she wasn't the type of mom to bury her head in the sand. She would want them to be safe.

"I've told you where I'll be and when I'm expected home. That's all you need to know." With a little squeeze, she released him. "I'll go get my purse and coat."

Delilah followed her mother out of the room. Felix stepped forward, toe to toe with Cash. Caught on the cusp of manhood, he was slim and lithe, with only the promise of bulk in his broad shoulders.

"I Googled you." His tone was low and threatening, though his eyes darted nervously. "I know you went to jail."

"So does your mother." Cash didn't expect the young man to *like* him, but he hoped Penta's protector would understand he'd never put her in danger. That he hadn't tricked or coerced her. "It was her decision not to tell you kids."

"Oh." Some of the belligerence evaporated from Felix's expression. "Well, that's good. I just wanted you to know I know."

"Appreciate you looking out for her. And I promise not to hurt her."

"Good." It appeared the conversation hadn't gone quite the way Felix had expected, but he wasn't done yet. "Make sure you don't. Or I'll be coming for you."

It should have been funny. Instead, Cash felt a sharp sweet burn at the back of his throat. For most of his life, he and his mother had been at odds, never seeing eye to eye, enjoying only tiny fragments of peaceful coexistence. She had died while he was in prison. In this moment, he had the desperate wish to see her once more, to have a chance to get to know her as a person, not a parent.

"I promise," he repeated. "I promise not to hurt your mother."

Delilah followed Penta into the mudroom near the back door. "You're going to have sex. I know it." She hugged her arms across her belly.

God, I hope so. All evening long, whenever Cash caught her eye, anticipation had rippled sparks through her blood and kept her cheeks rosier than the heat from the summer sun. She was ready for more.

Penta pulled on a light jacket. "You're smart enough to know that sex doesn't only happen when it's dark. Why is tonight different than all the afternoons Cash and I spent together?"

Delilah's scowl was an eerie imitation of Mark's. "You never go anywhere this late. What if something happens and we need you?"

It was the one argument that might have convinced Penta to change her mind—if she didn't know Delilah was a very capable, independent girl who thrived on responsibility.

"Sweetie." Penta brushed her palm over her daughter's short hair. "What's really bothering you?"

"It's bad enough Dad has a new wife, a new family." Tears shimmered in her brown eyes. "I never thought *you'd* leave us."

Penta sucked in a breath. Less than a month ago, this gut punch would have been an incentive to keep Cash at a distance, to focus on her family. But she was beginning to realize it wasn't healthy for a mother to have no life of her own. It wasn't good for her or her children.

"I'm not leaving you. I'm just"—she searched for the right words, fingers fluttering as she thought— "I'm just doing something for myself. I thought you were okay with me and Cash."

"I guess I didn't think it would, you know, mean you'd..." Her cheeks rosied.

"Have sex with him?" All the hairs on her body shivered to aroused attention. Others might look at Penta and see a prudish middle-aged mother. But she had enjoyed sex, at least during the first years of her marriage. Before it had become perfunctory and routine. Before Mark had stopped touching her all together. Before he'd accused her of being selfish and boring in bed.

"Maybe. I don't know. Yeah." Delilah bit her lip and stared at the floor.

"Just don't think about it, then," Penta instructed cheerfully, picking up her purse. "Remember, it's none of your business."

Back in the kitchen, Felix stood stiff and unyielding, and she caught a whiff of conflict searing the atmosphere. Cash shook his head in a tiny movement. She cast a worried glance at her son but took the hint.

"Okay then. I'll be back by midnight, like I said." She kissed Felix's cheek.

He jerked a nod, staring at Cash as if a conversation was still going on between them.

And suddenly, there was no more delay. The evening might have dragged like molasses, but the drive to Cash's shop flashed by in a blink. She followed his pickup into the alley and pulled into the slot beside him. With her heart tripping in her throat, she climbed out of her van and met him at the bottom of the stairs leading to his apartment on the second floor.

The security light above his head shadowed his face so she couldn't see his features clearly. He held out his hand and she gripped it.

"We don't have to do anything." His voice was harsh and gravelly, but the tenderness and honesty were impossible to ignore. "We can just talk, have a drink."

Holding tight—to both her courage and his hand— she led him up the stairs and paused on the landing so he could unlock the door. "I don't want to talk. I don't want a drink. I want you. In bed."

With Penta gripping his right hand, Cash had difficulty getting the key in the lock with his left. It didn't help that both his hands were trembling and his head spun dizzily.

Hearing her state—defiantly and definitely—that she wanted to be with him was more intoxicating than the strongest whiskey. He didn't drink hard liquor anymore but hadn't forgotten its powerful seductive pull.

It was nothing compared to Penta's impact.

His apartment was lit only by the glow of the light outside the window that looked onto the street. Blue shadows gathered in the corners and veiled the walls. The click of the refrigerator motor echoed loudly.

"How long have you lived here?" Her eyes reflected a liquid sheen as her gaze swept the space— small galley kitchen to the left, living room straight ahead—

—door leading to the bedroom on the right.

"Almost nine years. When I got out, I needed to rebuild my business. I rented a garage, slept in the back, cooked with a microwave. Ate a lot of soup." He smiled wryly at the memory. Transitioning out of the system had been tough. Not falling back into old habits had been even tougher. Somehow, he'd managed. "A couple years later, a mechanic I knew decided to retire, wanted someone to buy his place. I could afford the payment—barely—but still couldn't afford both the shop and a place to live. So, I moved in up here. It wasn't an apartment, of course. I fixed it up slowly, whenever I had a little cash."

"It's nice." At his dismissive snort, Penta shook their joined hands. "No, I mean it. Cozy, efficient, neat, and tidy. Just like your shop."

His heart swelled at her compliment, which terrified him. Having Penta's approval meant he could lose it.

She studied the floor-to-ceiling bookshelf he'd built. It took up the entire front wall, framing the wide window. "That's a lot of books. I didn't know you liked to read."

He hadn't, not until he'd gone to jail. Then he'd discovered words could take him out of his cell, away from his enforced routine, shield him from the grim realities of prison. He didn't say any of that to Penta, just grunted an acknowledgement.

"Is that the bedroom?" She nodded toward the open door through which a dresser and nightstand were visible.

Answering with action rather than words, he led her in. Another window overlooked the street, and cold white light fell onto the blue and red plaid bedspread. He'd always had a tendency toward neatness, which prison had hardened into an unbreakable custom. Compared to Penta's cluttered, lived-in, well-used home, his tidiness seemed grim and forbidding.

"I'm a little nervous." The words rushed from her

in a clipped cascade. "It's been a while for me."

"Me too." Longer than a while. He'd tried to be "normal," to meet people, make friends, maybe find someone to love. But his past kept getting in the way, and he'd stopped trying years ago.

Until Penta. What had begun as a ruse had become so much more.

"And I'm not exactly..." She waggled her free hand at her body in a self-deprecating motion. "I mean, I've had four kids."

"You are beautiful. Your body is beautiful." Not that he'd seen much of it yet. Tonight, that would change. Drawing her to the bed, he sat down and pulled her onto his lap. "Remember. We can stop any time. *Any* time. You got that?"

She nodded, brown eyes huge.

Cupping her face in his palms, he kissed her forehead, letting his lips slide over the crease lines between her brows. Her breath whooshed out in a sigh, fluttering against his neck. He wondered if she could feel his cock stiffening.

He feathered her chin and cheeks with his whiskers before meeting her mouth with his. Her hands gripped his shoulders, and she shifted so she was straddling him.

He fell into her kiss like a stone plummeting into the dark depths of a well.

Chapter Eighteen

Penta threaded her fingers through Cash's hair, the strong planes of his skull smooth under her palms. Their mouths nipped and teased, licked and clung, the choreography excitingly familiar yet deliciously new.

At the back of her mind, a voice whispered they should stop before things went too far, that she would bore him as she'd bored Mark. She appreciated the tact that had spurred Cash to call her beautiful, but she knew who she was, what she looked like—

She slapped duct tape over that timid creature's mouth.

Calloused hands slid under the hem of her shirt and rested on her hips, thumbs brushing the soft skin of her stomach, the underside of her breasts. Tonight, she would be Penta Unleashed. She would savour and remember every moment. If this was her only chance to be with Cash, she wouldn't squander it.

He drew back, eyes heavy-lidded, cheekbones stark. "I want to see you naked."

Heart thundering, she wriggled out of her jacket and let it fall behind her. His hands trailed up her torso, bumping over the bulges her bra raised in the flesh under her arms, and dragged her oversized T-shirt off.

Reaching behind her, he struggled briefly with the clasp, all the while kissing her jaw, her neck. It was a fine distraction from the knowledge he would soon be uncovering her four-baby breasts. He grunted as the hooks let go and lifted his head, fingers already at the straps on her shoulders.

He peeled the bra from her, slow and tantalizing, his gaze locked on what he revealed. "Pretty." He thumbed her nipples and her back arched. "Silky. Warm."

Her arousal spiked at his obvious satisfaction. Rocking her hips into the ridge behind his jeans, she tugged at his shirt. "Now you."

He ignored her, kissing the imprints her bra had branded onto her shoulders, fingers busy on her breasts. She moaned. "Please, Cash. Please." She wanted more. She wanted everything.

With a growl, he reared back, whipping off his shirt. Before she had a chance to see anything, he wrapped his arms around her and twisted, somehow managing to haul them both further up the bed so she was stretched out across its width.

He rose above her, braced on his hands and knees. "Please what?"

She ignored the question, fascinated by the marvellously thick pelt of hair covering his chest. Raising her head, she buried her nose in it and inhaled. Cash's scent—cinnamon, fresh air, and was that gear oil?—made her dizzy. Arousal heated her core, melted her thoughts. Her head dropped back to the mattress, and she took another long, slow look.

A chain tattoo led from one shoulder to the other just under his collarbones. She caught glimpses of more ink on his ribcage. Her fingers swept up his pecs, down his sides, teased at his waistband.

He caught her hand, tugged it over her head. "Please what, Penta."

"Hmm?" It was the best she could do, her mouth dry with lust, her brain dazed with his overwhelming presence. Her free hand wandered lower, and he captured that too. She wriggled, unexpectedly enjoying the determined yet delicate restraint.

"Tell me what you want."

Distracted from her survey of his body, she looked at his face. He observed her with such glittering intensity she lost her breath. "What?"

"Tell me what you want, then beg me for more. I want to hear you scream my name."

Her body liquefied. Drowning in sensuality, she struggled to speak.

"Tell me what you want, Penta," Cash commanded for the third time.

Had no one ever asked her what she wanted before?

Penta's obvious bewilderment created a maelstrom of conflicting emotions in Cash. Rage that her needs had been ignored in the past. Delight that he'd be the one to fulfill those needs.

Nuzzling her neck, the sensitive skin under her ear, he softened his tone, barely breathing the words. "Where should I touch you? Where do you want my mouth?"

The pulse at the base of her throat throbbed rapidly. He licked it and she jolted, hands curling into fists. He was hyperaware of her blood rushing through the veins of her wrists, pinned by his much larger hands.

Her voice, when it finally came, was thin and hesitant, with a lilt that warned him not to press too hard, too fast. "My breasts?"

He hummed with contentment and dropped tiny kisses from her throat up the slope of her full breast to the rosy circle around her nipple. Her body tightened. When he moved away from the sensitive centre to the shallow valley between, she whimpered as if disappointed. Swiping his tongue on the underside, he revelled in the softness, the scent of summery sweat, before making his way back up again.

With her arms still held above her head and his knees clamped around her legs, all she could do was squirm. Her breasts jiggled in delightful temptation.

"More?" His lips brushed her nipple as he spoke.

She moaned. "More. Everything. All of you."

His cock, crushed inside his jeans, jerked in painful agreement. Relinquishing her hands, he unbuttoned and unzippered, groaning in relief, before latching onto her breast again, hunching over her smaller form.

She tasted of honey and heat, of home and heart. He plumped the mounds of fragrant flesh together and feasted on one then the other. She made quiet, needy sounds as her hands swept from his skull down his chest, around his ribs, and lower. Her fingers slipped inside his unfastened jeans and gripped his hips.

He showed his approval by nipping her with lip-covered teeth. She gasped and arched—and one hand slid between them to grip his cock.

Her fingers were cool and firm. With no hesitancy, she worked him up and down, thumb and forefinger making a ring that bumped over the head of his swollen shaft in erotic torture. Panting, he raised his head. "If you keep doing that..." Helplessly, he thrust into her hand. His balls tightened with impending release, but he couldn't tear himself out of her clasp.

"Yes. I need you inside me." Her fierce command revealed nothing but need and desire, all shyness gone. "I have condoms in my purse."

"Got some here." He yanked open the nightstand drawer, fumbling for the slippery foil packet. "Move up."

She scrambled on elbows and heels until she rested against the pillows at the head of the bed. In one swift yank, he pulled off her underwear and leggings. The next time he would take more care, spend more time. But by the rose on her face, the way her knees fell open, she was as eager as he. Musky scent filled his nostrils, and he sucked in a deep breath as he struggled out of his own clothing.

Kneeling before her, he rolled on the condom. Her

arms reached for him. "Come here. Now."

It took a moment or two to get the angle right, to sort out whose limbs went where. When he slid into her warm welcome, he almost wept.

She whispered in his ear, meaningless syllables suffused with delight and passion. With one elbow braced by her head and the other arm under her hips, he thrust in a staccato rhythm, lost in acceptance, in joy, in connection.

A shudder swept through her and her legs stiffened as liquid heat rushed over his cock. Moments later, his own release shattered, pinwheels of light exploding behind his eyes, electric shocks jolting down his spine.

Penta lay panting and limp under Cash's sprawling weight, extremities tingling from the force of her orgasm. Good god, she'd needed that. She had a toy—ordered online and delivered in discreet packaging—hidden at the back of her nightstand, but rarely used it.

Nothing inanimate could possibly compare to what Cash had just given her.

As her skin cooled and her breathing eased, doubt crept back in. Had she been too forward? Or not forward enough? Should she have touched him longer, maybe even offered a blow job? It wasn't her favourite sexual activity, though she might not mind it with Cash. But he'd said he wanted her to ask for what she'd wanted, and she'd *really* wanted him inside her. Hopefully, he had meant it.

His torso swelled as he drew in a long breath, crushing her deeper into the mattress, and then he listed to the side. She wanted to go with him, to cuddle under his arm, drape her knee over his thighs, but didn't want to appear clingy.

The growl of a heavy engine reverberated through the exterior wall, the beams of headlights tracking across the ceiling. "I'll be right back." He rolled off the mattress and disappeared toward the bathroom.

Now what? Should she get up and go? Midnight was still a couple hours away, but she didn't think she could stand the awkwardness of small talk. Not after the intensity, the intimacy, of what had just passed between them.

Before she could decide, he returned and stretched out beside her.

"I'm sorry."

She blinked and turned her head toward him, her hair rasping on the pillow. "What?" Icy hands clutched her throat. Was he already regretting what they'd done?

His profile was limned by the indirect glow of the streetlight outside the window—heavy brow, pugnacious nose, jutting beard. "I should have taken more time. Shouldn't have rushed things."

She wasn't sure how to interpret that. "Was it me? Did I force you to...finish...too soon?"

He propped himself up on his elbow, grey eyes black in the dimness. "I told you to ask for what you wanted. And when you did? Fuck." His tone was reverent. "I couldn't say no. Still, I should have taken the time to make sure you were ready."

Her grinding sense of insecurity vanished. Mirth burbled in to replace it. "Oh, I was ready. I've been ready all evening."

"It's lucky I didn't know that." His attention sharpened, lasering in on her and her alone. "Do you have any idea what it does to me, to hear you say you want me?"

"I think I do." She gripped the back of his neck and levered herself up so she could kiss the tip of his nose. "Because I feel the same way about you. Knowing I made you lose your head—" She didn't hold back her confident grin.

He lay back, snaked an arm under her, and tugged her close. She rested her head on his shoulder and sighed long and luxuriously.

"What's that for?"

Too many answers came to mind. She chose the simplest, his chest hair tickling her lips as she spoke. "Just comfy. I like your bed."

"I like having you in it."

The words seemed to surprise him as much as they surprised her if the sudden stiffening of his body was anything to go by.

Afraid of the emotions yawing through her heart, the precipice of desire she clung to, she remained quiet. For several minutes, there was nothing but Cash's fingers toying with her hair, her palm registering the thud of his heart, and the silence humming through the room.

Reluctant to outstay her welcome, she whispered into his skin, "I suppose I should go."

"No." She yipped as he surged off the mattress and loomed over her. "You have more than an hour before you promised the kids you'd be home. I may not be as young as I used to be, but I've been saving up for a long time."

She didn't think biology worked that way but couldn't help the burst of affectionate lust. "Are you saying you're ready for a second course?"

"Not yet." He crawled down her body and spread her legs. "But an appetizer will take care of that."

Chapter Nineteen

Cash wasn't sure what to expect after Saturday night. He knew what he *wanted*—more time alone with Penta—but he wouldn't presume that's what she wanted too.

His desire for her hadn't waned. In fact, it grew with every day that passed—every frustrating, cock-blocked day.

It wasn't just that she was occupied by the busyness of her family's life. It was the logistics of having an affair with a mother of four. He wasn't sure he'd be able to get it up at her place, knowing Abra and Delilah were across the hall. And she couldn't be continually coming to his place for a quick fuck. What he felt for her was more honest than that, more sincere.

They saw each other daily. Now it was summer break, Cyril was spending most of his time completing the last hours of his penance. Penta often came in for a few minutes during drop off and pick up, but they'd managed to sneak no more than hurried, breathless kisses. By the time Friday rolled around, Cash was itching to get her out of her clothes again.

He left the storeroom, where he'd been conducting inventory while distracted by a daydream about a naked Penta bent over the arm of his sofa, and braked to a sudden stop one stride inside the main room. Elle and Cyril stood near the front window, heads close together in an attitude of conspiracy. The sight banished the remnants of his fantasy, and he took a half-step back into the shadows of the hall.

When Linda hadn't stormed into his shop in the days following his apology to Elle, he'd begun to hope she'd accepted his presence in their daughter's life. It was a fragile, tentative hope, but stronger than any he'd had before and nourished by Elle's new habit of dropping by the shop several days a week. They'd even exchanged phone numbers, so they no longer had to depend on her mother to relay messages.

Elle giggled, stared shyly at the floor, and tucked her hair behind her ear. Cash frowned. Was she *flirting* with Cyril? What about the kid he'd thrown against the fence?

He couldn't hear what they were saying. They stood in profile on the far side of the shop where Cyril was supposed to be restocking shelves. The boy's scrawny shoulders were straight and square, unlike his usual slumped, slothful stance and he couldn't take his eyes off Elle.

Driven by protective instinct, he strode forward. "Elle. When did you get here?" He hadn't meant to speak loudly, but his voice boomed against the concrete walls.

The teenagers jerked apart as if pulled by strings. Cyril blushed bright red, the whiteheads of acne showing up sharp on his cheeks.

Elle lifted her chin in Linda's familiar gesture. "Just a minute ago."

"Hmm." He raised an eyebrow at Cyril, who began placing bottles of motor oil on the shelf with an air of nervous inattention.

"I wanted to say goodbye. Mom and I are going to Gramma and Gramps' cabin for the long weekend. She's waiting outside." She jerked a thumb toward the street. Through the glass, Linda was visible sitting at the wheel of her car. He couldn't read her expression and wondered if the fact she hadn't come in was a good or bad sign. "On Tuesday, we're driving to

Vancouver. We'll be there for a week." She slid a glance toward Cyril, her expression full of wistful longing.

Apprehension shuddered through Cash like a ride on a washboard road. He wasn't the only one she'd come to say goodbye to. Maybe wasn't even the most important one. Ignoring that revelation for the moment, he nodded. "Have a good time."

"We will. Mom's got friends down there we visit every summer and it's always fun. But I'm hoping we can check out some college campuses. I don't graduate for a couple of years, but it's never too early to start looking, right?"

Loss swept over him. He barely knew his daughter and she was already moving away. "What about UNBC?" The local university had a stellar reputation.

"Oh, I still might. But I want to see what else is out there."

God, she sounded so grown up. He had missed so much of her life. Regret gnawed at him. It was his own fault, of course. He should have fought harder to get to know her, tried sooner to convince Linda he'd reformed, that he wasn't the danger they both knew he was.

No. Not *was*. Had been. He wasn't that man anymore. Penta believed in him. He needed to start believing in himself.

"That's smart." He harrumphed, trying to clear his throat of the swirling emotions, but his voice still came out gruff and gravelly. "Come see me when you get back. Tell me all about it."

He wanted to hug her, but it was a liberty he hadn't taken since the disastrous birthday party. Maybe she saw his yearning, as she stepped forward and squeezed him tight. "I will. See you later."

With another quick look at the silent Cyril, she left the shop, climbed in beside Linda, and was gone.

Drawing in a calming breath, Cash turned to the youth. "All right. What's going on with you and Elle?"

One shoulder hunched up under his ear. "Nothing."

"She has a boyfriend."

"Not anymore. He broke it off. After—" He slid an uneasy glance over his shoulder.

"After I tossed him on his ass." One more sin to lay at his feet. It was a wonder Elle was speaking to him.

"Yeah. Elle says he was a jerk, anyway."

If that was the case, why was she going out with him in the first place? He decided not to go there. "So. You and Elle?"

"We talk. It's nothing." The boy fidgeted with the bottles he'd placed on the shelf, lining them up with finicky precision. "Can I ask you something?"

Cash's heart tumbled to the pit of his stomach. He didn't think Cyril's question had anything to do with motorcycle oil. "What?"

"Elle told me you went to jail. She says you beat up a guy, almost killed him."

The air went sticky, trapping Cash like a fly in a puddle of fuel. He'd hoped volunteering at the youth-at-risk centre and being forced to discuss this exact subject would make it easier. It hadn't. He wasn't sure he'd ever be comfortable talking about why he went to prison. But he'd come to know Cyril pretty well over the last few weeks, and the kid only spoke up when it was important. He hissed a breath in between his teeth. "What's your question?"

Cyril moved a container a millimetre to the right. "Why'd you do it? Beat him up?"

The kid couldn't look him in the eye, but Cash didn't think he was scared. He had the oddest feeling Cyril was looking for...permission? "What's going on? Are you in trouble?"

"Nah. Well, maybe." He pressed his fingertips on the edge of the metal shelves, like he was doing standing push-ups. "The guys who were with me...you know. That night? They got a grudge against this other guy. Want me to come along, teach him a lesson."

Ice shards filled his lungs. "You still hanging with those idiots?"

"I tried to stay away. But we had a lot of classes together at school. Besides"—his tone pleaded for understanding—"they're my friends."

He'd had "friends" like that too. Friends who had *not* had his best interests at heart.

Usually, he pushed memories of that night away, refused to let them get a grip. In this moment, he let them come. Felt again the vicious joy of battle, the icy calm of rage.

The desperate horror when the berserk fog lifted, and he realized what he'd done.

"Want to know why I beat up that guy? I was drinking with some buddies in a bar. Probably had a couple too many. Not that I was so drunk I didn't know what I was doing. Just too drunk to be smart. He bumped into me, said some shit about it being my fault. Made me mad, and my so-called buddies said I should teach him a lesson, just like yours. Said I shouldn't let him disrespect me like that. Still, I might have let it slide, but he threw the first punch. He was about my size and raring to go. After that"—he shrugged and the ghost of old bruises and cracked ribs made him wince—"well, it's pretty much a blur. I guess I caught him a good one and he fell back, hit his head on the corner of the bar. That's what almost killed him."

If it had been Cash's first offense, he might have gotten off with a lighter sentence. But he'd been known to the cops since he was about Cyril's age. Shoplifting, vandalism, a brawl or two between rival gangs. Maybe if someone had got him into Camp Chance...maybe if just one of the cops he'd met hadn't been an officious asshole...maybe then his life would have been different.

Maybes were a bitch.

It was so quiet he could hear the voices of a couple passing by on the sidewalk. Cyril stared at the bottles of motorcycle oil, still and silent.

"I'm not blaming anyone but myself for what I did." Cash felt brittle with regret, a regret he would never lose. "But I might not have done it if my buddies hadn't egged me on. No one needs friends like that, Cyril. No one."

He spun on his heel and sought refuge in the storeroom once more.

Penta pulled up just down the street from Cash's shop, turned off the ignition, and slouched in her seat. She needed a few moments to rebuild her cheerful façade and had deliberately parked out of sight.

She'd spent the afternoon dropping off resumes. Her online applications had borne no fruit, so she'd decided to try in person. Unfortunately—yet perhaps inevitably—she had the same results, with the added insult of being rejected to her face. One acned manager at a clothing store had actually laughed.

Even more depressing than today's humiliations was the growing realization that she didn't want any of the jobs she was qualified for. She needed something to fill the coming void when her children were grown and gone, but stocking shelves or answering phones held no attraction. Was she naïve to hope she might find a position that would allow her to rediscover the young woman who'd enjoyed solving chemistry problems and exploring the fascinating world of physics?

She dragged herself out of her van and down the sidewalk. Cyril was the only person in view when she entered the shop. He stood next to a stack of shelving, staring at the hall that led to the rear, a puzzled look on his face, a cardboard box at his feet.

"Hey, sweetie. Ready to go?"

"Yeah. Just got to put this away." He picked up the carton but stayed where he was.

"Is Cash in the back? I'll let him know we're

leaving." A few moments with him would brighten her day. Not that she would bore him with her troubles. She had to deal with that on her own. She took two steps toward the hall, but Cyril stopped her.

"He might be a little upset."

Alarm raised the hairs on her neck. "What happened? Was Linda here again?"

He shook his head. "No." Then he added in a rush, "Did you know he was in jail because he beat up a guy?"

"Oh." She'd decided to tell her kids about Cash's past only if it became necessary. While their relationship was no longer just for show, she wasn't kidding herself that it was permanent. "Actually, yes, I did. Not the details, but the general gist."

"I don't get it." Cyril seemed sincerely confused. "He's a tough guy, but he's not mean. I've never seen him mad."

The angriest Penta had ever seen Cash was the night he'd brought Cyril home. Though she'd been wary of him then, she'd never felt in danger. But she'd seen the aftermath of his fury at Elle's birthday party and had no doubt he'd be formidable in a temper. "I imagine he works hard to keep his cool since he knows how awful the consequences can be."

"Yeah." He flipped the box over and over in his hands thoughtfully. "Is it okay if I walk home today? Sorry you came all this way."

She didn't know what startled her more—the fact he wanted to walk home, which would take more than an hour, or that he'd apologized. In one of those rare scintillatingly clear moments that life sometimes offered, her view of Cyril...switched. Whether it was the way he was carrying himself or simply the expression on his face, she couldn't say. Suddenly he was no longer a boy but a young man.

"Is everything okay?" She rubbed his shoulder gently.

He didn't shrug off her concern as he usually did,

instead offering her a serious, diffident smile. "Yeah. I just have some thinking to do. I'll bring this back, get my pack, and let Cash know you're here."

He vanished, reappeared a minute later, gave her a kiss on the cheek—which floored her yet again—and was gone.

Chapter Twenty

Penta hesitated, undecided whether she should wait for Cash or search him out. A moment later, he strode into the room.

Her welcoming smile faltered at the cool blankness in his tombstone-grey eyes. Gone was her intense lover, her passionate protector. In his place was the grim, stoic loner she'd first met.

He walked past with barely a glance. Locking the front door, he took a wide detour around her, heading for the corner where he did his real work. The motorcycle he was restoring had been pushed to the side and a modern monster with hard-sided carriers, supple leather seats, and well-tended chrome sat, proud and arrogant, in the middle of the stained concrete.

"Cyril said he was walking home. You should go too." The words dropped with icy precision from his lips.

She shivered and shuffled forward, her heart choking her. "What's going on, Cash?"

"Your sons know I went to jail." He hadn't picked up a tool, hadn't made any movement toward the bike propped like a wall between them.

"Both of them?" That hadn't been on her radar at all. She blinked, adjusting to the revelation. "Cyril just told me he knows, but Felix does too?"

"He confronted me after the barbeque, before we came here."

"Oh." The choking sensation intensified. "I was hoping they'd have time to get to know you before I told them." *If I ever did.* Guilt prickled. Was she more ashamed of Cash's past than she was willing to acknowledge?

He shifted his weight from foot to foot in an anxious tell she'd never witnessed before. "This isn't going to work."

She scanned the area, looking for somewhere to sit, her knees shaky. The best she could find was a large square box that declared it contained Super Absorbent Paper Towels. It squished alarmingly beneath her butt. "What isn't going to work?"

He gestured to her and then tapped his own chest. "This. Us."

She wasn't in love with Cash. She couldn't be. The fissure in her chest wasn't heartbreak. "I don't understand."

"We come from two different worlds, Penta. It's a cliché because it's true. I almost killed a man in a barroom brawl. I went to jail, for fuck's sake, and I deserved to." His voice broke, his cold expression shattering into fragments of pain.

Her own agony eased in the face of his. "I know that. I've known it all along. Why does it matter now? What did my boys say?"

He gripped his beard with both hands, tugging. "Felix is worried about you."

But not Cyril? If her second son hadn't accosted Cash on her behalf, what was he doing bringing up the topic? Casual but cruel curiosity?

"That's sweet. But it's not necessary." Cautiously, as if approaching a stray dog, she stood up and rounded the bike with slow, deliberate steps. "I know you'd never hurt me."

She repressed a jolt of surprise when, with explosive violence, he pounded his fists on the workbench, making the tools jump and clatter. "Damn right I wouldn't. You can't blame them for thinking it, though. And what about your father? What happens when he finds out?" He pressed his knuckles to the surface with all his weight.

She rested her hand flat on his back. The muscles were rigid under her palm. "He knows, Cash. I told him before the party."

He stood still under her touch. Then his shoulders sank, and his head dropped. "He never said anything. We talked a long time. He never said anything."

"He's a firm believer in redemption, for letting a person's present actions speak louder than past sins." *And so am I.* She sternly banished the last sliver of shame she'd been harbouring. Cash worked so hard to be a better man. She refused to be embarrassed about his history. Wrapping her arms around his waist, she laid her cheek on his back and listened to the thudding of his heart. "I'm proud of you, Cash. You should be too."

Cash hadn't realized how disturbed he'd been by Cyril's question until he'd spewed his agitation all over Penta. As soon as he'd seen her, though, all he'd wanted to do was bury his head in her lap and howl out his remorse and regret.

At least he hadn't blurted out Cyril's reason for bringing up the topic. He wouldn't betray the boy's secret unless he absolutely had to.

He inhaled deeply several times, the clasp of her arms around his torso as comforting as a weighted blanket. "Sorry for losing it."

Her breath huffed out in a quiet chuckle. "I have teenagers. That was downright reserved compared to their meltdowns."

"You really told your dad about me *before* we met?"

"I did. In hindsight, we probably should have told the kids too."

Her use of *we* melted the last chunks of panic from

his chest. He shifted so he could wrap his arms around her shoulders and curl over her. She snuggled in. For a few minutes, they did nothing but hold each other.

As his pulse settled, his libido woke up. He gave his cock a stern talking to, but it ignored him.

Penta lifted her head and let her lower body rest heavily against his. "Well, hello there." The amused glint in her brown eyes burned with heat. Her palms teased under the hem of his T-shirt and slid up his pecs.

He groaned. "You probably don't have enough time—" His words broke off with a hiss as she tugged one nipple.

"No. Not right now." She rucked up the material and dropped a kiss on his chest, then shot a guilty glance at the front windows where passersby had a wide screen view. Smoothing the shirt back into place, she gave a wistful sigh. "I can't stop thinking about last week. I want to be with you again, I really do. You're being remarkably patient."

He could only grunt in reply as his hands moved restlessly on her back, tweaking the curls at the nape of her neck. He'd never realized how potent the combination of easy affection and lustful sensuality could be.

"I just had a thought." She popped up on her toes, nipped his lip, and dropped back onto her heels. "The girls are staying with Mark for the long weekend. Felix is out of town, going to a concert in Vancouver with friends. Only Cyril and I will be home. If you wanted..." She traced the Harley Davidson logo on his T-shirt with a delicate finger and then finished in a rush, not meeting his eyes. "You could spend the weekend with us. And I wouldn't mind...I mean, I would like it if..." Again, she trailed off.

"Are you asking me to stay the nights?"

She peeped up at him. "If you want. If you don't think it will be too awkward. But you know Cyril best and he knows—"

This time, her words were cut off by his mouth. He kissed her with a passion that burned like a fever. "I want, Penta," he murmured against her lips. "Holy Christ, I want."

Penta spent the long weekend alternately burning with embarrassment, suffused with contentment, and overflowing with delicious wickedness.

Cash arrived just before dinner on Saturday. The three of them took their places at the table with excruciating politeness. Conversation started off stilted and she despaired of finding a topic that would encourage Cyril to break his morose silence. But the metamorphosis she'd witnessed the day before seemed to be continuing. When she mentioned the new release in an action movie franchise she knew he liked, he brightened, and soon he and Cash were deep into dissecting how the stunts had been done and lambasting the lead's mediocre acting.

Afterward, the three of them streamed an earlier movie in the same series. Cyril sprawled in an armchair while she and Cash almost-but-not-quite cuddled on the sofa. It ended about the time the neighbourhood association was set to launch their Canada Day fireworks, so they walked to the nearby park and oohed and aahed along with the crowd.

When they returned to the house, Cyril hesitated at the top of the stairs leading to his room in the basement. His gaze flicked between her and Cash, a worldly wisdom in his eyes that made her want to squirm. For several painful seconds their roles were reversed, as if she were the child and he the parent. She wondered why it was worse with Cyril than it had been with Delilah and Felix.

He nodded at Cash. "I guess I'll see you in the morning. Goodnight, Mom." His feet thudded down the stairs and she heard the quiet click of his door closing.

Cash turned to her, expression blazing with shameless intent. "Seems like we have his blessing."

Her mouth too dry to speak, she simply took his hand and led him to her bedroom.

Like their first time together, the sex was fervent and volatile, fueled by extreme unspoken emotions. She fell asleep curled under his arm and woke later to the sweep of his hand over her belly, her breasts. This time, their lovemaking was tender, drowsy, a matter of soft words and sipping lips, quiet pulses and rolling tides.

The next day and night passed with an aura of unreality. It was the same sensation she had during vacations—that the real world was on pause and the usual rules didn't apply. Whenever the little voice inside her brain reminded her this was nothing but an interlude, she silenced it firmly.

The hours went by far too quickly. Cash left on Monday afternoon after a gratifyingly lustful but disappointingly quick romp on the kitchen counter, Cyril being out of the house at the time. Felix wasn't expected home until around eight o'clock, but Mark pulled into the driveway at dinnertime. The girls piled out, chattering excitedly even before they swept into the house, their father bringing up the rear.

"Guess what, Mom!" Abra danced on her toes, bobbing with delight. "Daddy wants to take us to Mexico!"

"He does? When?" Many northerners fled south to enjoy beach vacations in the depths of winter. It was a little early to start planning, but she should be thankful Mark had given her this much notice.

Delilah's enthusiasm was only slightly restrained by her teenage ennui. "Jacinta's family have invited us to come for the whole month of August. They live in this village near Manzanillo." She enunciated the word with a Spanish inflection no doubt learned from her stepmother. "She showed us pictures. It looks cool."

Penta stared at Mark, brain reeling. "A whole month? And so soon?"

"The boys are invited, too." He didn't even have the grace to look ashamed. He shouldn't have mentioned it to *any* of the children without talking to Penta first.

She clenched her fists in fury. If she expressed opposition now, she'd be the spoilsport, hated and despised. "That sounds very exciting," she said through gritted teeth. "Your father and I will have to discuss it."

Thankfully, neither of the girls took this as a possible *no*. They clambered up the stairs to their rooms, leaving Penta facing an unrepentant ex-husband.

"You know you should have talked to me before raising the girls' hopes."

"What reason could you have for not allowing them to go?" His chin jutted in challenge. "They're old enough to know their own minds, even Abra. Jacinta and I chose August so as not to disrupt the school year. I don't imagine Felix will go"—she thought she saw disappointment flicker across his features—"but hopefully Cyril does. It will be a great experience for all of them."

She hated he was right. Hated he'd considered all the angles. Hated that she hoped his guess regarding Felix was correct, as it was petty to wish their oldest son would reject his father in even the slightest way.

But most of all she hated that she *wanted* to say no.

Chapter Twenty-One

Rainbow Park, an urban refuge of rolling green hills and copses of coniferous trees, was a favourite location for wedding photos in the summer and tobogganing in the winter. On this Saturday in July, a large bowl-shaped area was dotted with colourful tents and displays, and several food trucks had made their careful way down the slope. The scent of burgers and hotdogs mingled with that of samosas and souvlaki, and the laughter of children floated over the babble of the crowd.

Rainbow colours flew everywhere—flags and banners, T-shirts and dresses, hats and bandannas—as the Prince George Pride Society and their community supporters celebrated with family and friends.

The Silverberry Book Club members were out in full force. It wasn't their official July activity—that would be a yoga class on the riverbank the following morning—but Terrance Renfrew and his husband Bennett Ayers were on the organizing committee and nothing short of an earthquake would have stopped the Silverberries from coming.

At the moment, most of them were gathered in a loose group on the soft springy lawn on the side of a hill, watching the commotion below.

Helen shuffled closer to Penta, careless of grass stains on her denim shorts. "Where did that man of yours get to?"

She wriggled at the idea of Cash being *her man.* "He's in the lineup for ice cream." She pointed to a snaking queue that led to a truck serving flavours that included matcha tea, poached pear with goat cheese, and honey lavender.

Helen nudged her with an elbow. "It's nice to see you happy."

She considered this statement. "Does that mean I didn't look happy before?"

In her usual exuberant style, Helen was decked out in rainbows from her socks to her headband. The sequined arc on her T-shirt glittered and flashed in the sun. "Not like this. Not relaxed and content. And if I may say so, well-pleasured."

Penta's flush seared her cheeks. "Helen!"

"What are you embarrassed about? It takes one to know one." She smiled fondly at her husband, Nathan, currently in deep discussion with Dr. Rafe Talbot. Rafe had come with Natalie Minton, a long-time member of the Silverberries. Penta wasn't sure about the stern-faced man yet. He seemed rather dour and unfriendly, especially compared to the bubbly Natalie. But he'd been present when Lynn—sitting a little further down the hill with her husband Benjamin and their toddler and infant sons—went into shockingly fast labour a couple months ago. Despite being a pathologist and not an obstetrician, he had handled the situation marvellously. Penta was giving him the benefit of the doubt. For now.

"It's different for you. You knew Nathan for years before you got together. Cash and I met barely a month ago. We have nothing in common." The doubts she was constantly battling swarmed like black flies. "Honestly, I don't know what I'm doing with him. What *he's* doing with *me.*"

"Stop that. You are a lovely woman with plenty to offer any man. Do you like him?"

"I do." She didn't have to think about it, not even for an instant.

"Then just relax, see where things go."

Nathan approached and held out his hand to Helen. "The lineup at the churro station is as short as it's going to get. Come with me?"

"Of course!" She bounced to her feet, gripped his hand, and the couple headed down the slope, passing Terrance as he made his way slowly upward.

He joined Penta, lowering himself carefully to the grass, and let out a deep sigh. "I hate sitting on the ground, but my feet are killing me."

"How are things going?"

"Very well. The usual hiccups, of course, but nothing insurmountable."

Unlike Helen, Terrance's homage to the day's theme was a striped silk scarf tied loosely around his neck and a small pin on the collar of his pale blue polo shirt. How he managed to preserve the knife-edge crease in his khaki dress shorts she would never know. "Where's Bennett?"

She watched his response with sharp attention. They'd spoken a few times since the motorcycle lesson, when he'd first hinted there was tension in his marriage. She'd been waiting for him to bring it up again, but he hadn't, and he didn't do so now.

"Dealing with a porta-potty emergency." He shuddered.

She decided a gentle prod wouldn't be out of line. "And you guys are...okay?"

Terrance stared over the crowd, his eyes unfocused. "We're going to counselling. I think it's helping."

"Good. Good for you both. If there's anything I can do..."

"There isn't, but thank you. We have to work through this ourselves. I am more hopeful than I was a month ago." He patted her knee briskly. "What about you? How is that brood of yours?"

"Mark wants to take the girls to Mexico for August. To stay with Jacinta's family." She had thought of little else all week.

"That sounds exciting." Which was exactly what Cash had said when she'd mentioned it to him. Both had also used the same dry tone, apparently knowing without being told she didn't like the idea. "What about the boys?"

"He invited them, of course. But they said no." She tried not to sound smug, as she doubted she was the reason Felix and Cyril had rejected the offer. Still, the result was the same. She wouldn't be losing all her children to the lure of a far-off land.

"You'll let the girls go?"

Cash had reached the front of the line. "I don't want to. I know, I know, that's selfish. But a whole month? We used to spend every day of the summer together. It was our special time."

"You can't stop them from growing up, and seeing another way of life will be an excellent experience."

She sighed. "I have no good reason to refuse, and they'd hate me if I did. I just need some time to get used to the idea before I say yes." Below, Cash turned from the food truck with a cone in each hand and wound his way through the milling crowd toward her.

"I don't have children, so I can't fully understand what you're going through. But raising them to become independent is part of the job description, is it not?" Terrance flicked a speck of dirt off his shorts with a fastidious finger. "One of the things I've learned in counselling is that to have a healthy relationship with anyone else, you have to have a healthy one with yourself. Maybe you can take this time to reconnect with yourself as a woman, not only a mother."

His words were an echo of her own thoughts. That didn't make them any more welcome. "Easier said than done. They've been my entire focus for so long. I don't know if I can step back."

"What you need is something to occupy you. You could volunteer. Or find a job."

"Yeah. About that..." She plucked a blade of grass

and twirled it in her fingers.

"Penta." His neat eyebrows rose. "Have you been keeping secrets?"

Cash held the cones of whiskey caramel pecan and haskap berry at shoulder height as he dodged running, laughing children. Penta was seated where he'd left her, accompanied by a man about his own age. He remembered him from the motorcycle course. Trent? Terry? No, something more stick-up-the-ass. Terrance, that was it.

He was slim instead of broad, clean shaven instead of bearded, and dapper instead of scruffy. Basically, Cash's complete opposite. He might have felt threatened if Penta hadn't pointed out the man's husband earlier.

As he neared, he caught a few syllables of their conversation. He handed Penta her haskap cone and she tossed aside a mangled piece of grass before taking it. Then he sank down beside her, hips popping and complaining. "What's this about secrets?"

Her cheeks, already pink, reddened deeper. "It's not a secret. It's nothing at all, which is why I haven't mentioned it."

Terrance looked across Penta to Cash. "We were talking about her finding something to occupy her other than children and she got all flustered."

She swatted his arm with her free hand. "I did not get flustered. It's just—maybe I have been looking. For a job."

Terrance's cell phone rang, and he checked the screen. "Sorry, must run. They're about to start the costume parade and need wranglers. You can fill me in later." With a polite smile at Cash and a warmer one for Penta, he rose to his feet and sashayed down the hill.

Cash crunched a pecan, the almost-forgotten flavour of whiskey flooding his mouth as the ice cream melted on his tongue. "Why didn't you tell me?"

She rolled her shoulders. "I don't know. I feel rather ridiculous, looking for what is basically my first job at forty-four." She licked a trickle of melting treat off her knuckle, frowning at the cone like it was the cause of her embarrassment. "I have two years of science courses from university but no degree, no special qualifications, no sought-after skills."

"Science courses?" Scientists were nerdy, cold, and analytical, the inverse of Penta's sweetness, warmth, and compassion. Or so he'd always imagined.

"I thought I might work in a lab someday. Conducting experiments, solving puzzles." She nibbled at the edge of the waffle cone. "Mark and I met in university. I got pregnant and when we married, finishing my degree wasn't the most important thing in my life."

If Penta had brought the focus and attention she showered on her children to a career, she would have been an unstoppable force. "I'm sure you'll find something. You have more going for you than you think."

His attempt at consolation felt clunky and awkward, as if the emotional muscles necessary had atrophied. That's what happened when you kept to yourself, remained cut off from human contact as much as possible. Until one woman barged her way into your life and upset everything.

He tossed the last bite of cone into his mouth, stood up, and held out his hand. "I saw a temporary tattoo stand down below. Let's go get you inked."

Chapter Twenty-Two

Cash was greedy. That's all there was to it. Greedy for more of Penta's kisses, more of her lovemaking. More of *her*.

The time they spent together was never enough. He came to the gradual realization that it might never be enough. That he might want more of Penta than she could give. She had her children, her friends, her father, all of which filled her days.

While he had no one but her.

He rose from his crouch beside the Baby Bonnie, knees protesting. He'd had to put aside the Triumph's restoration for several days. This was always a busy time of year, with most bikes out of storage. Also, it didn't seem to matter that summer inevitably came after spring—there were always owners who were shocked it was July and demanded he rush to get their rides road ready so they could take advantage of the short northern British Columbia season.

Wiping his hands on a rag, he stared at the partially reconstructed bike. The longer he worked on it, the more attached he grew to the classic machine. As much as he liked having Penta ride pillion, maybe he should keep the Bonnie. In case Penta wanted to borrow her once in a while.

His thoughts drifted to Jeremy Wicken's, where she and the kids were having dinner. She'd invited him, like she did to almost everything, but he had said no. As much as he wanted to be with her, he wouldn't push his luck by accepting all her offers.

Which meant he had no one to blame but himself for his current solitary state.

Pissed off by his own whininess, he cleaned up his tools and headed to his apartment. Habit not hunger had him opening the fridge and staring at the contents. Though well-stocked, nothing tempted him into either cooking or eating.

If he stayed in tonight, he might just scratch his eyes out. Snatching up his leather jacket, he strode down the outside stairs, retrieved his bike from the lockup, and roared out of the alley.

He headed south, sweeping and swerving through the light traffic until he reached the main highway. Then, heedless of speed limits, he twisted the throttle and let the bike soar.

Half an hour later, the frantic rate had soothed his itchy soul. He coasted until he reached the proper pace, deciding he'd tempted fate enough. He'd been stopped for speeding once since he'd got out and had been put through the ringer before he was allowed on his way. He was in no mood to be polite to cops tonight.

Maybe it was that memory that sparked his next reckless impulse. Pulling a U-turn, he returned to the city and steered toward the rundown neighbourhood where he'd grown up. The late setting sun bathed the battered duplexes and ratty apartment buildings in oranges and pinks, highlighting their seedy appearance. A shudder rippled across his skin as the turmoil and frustration he'd experienced living there resurfaced with frightening ease.

He cruised past the last house his mother had rented. Weeds infested the yard, springing up undaunted between the deep ruts cut by the tires of the cars parked on it. The siding was peeled and warped, and a corner-to-corner crack in the front window was duct taped from the inside in a pathetic attempt at repair. He doubted it had looked much different when she'd occupied it. His mother had moved frequently from the time he was a child, but never to somewhere neat or safe or well-tended.

A compulsion he didn't want to examine drove him toward a low building with no windows and a heavy metal door. He pulled into the paved but potholed parking lot and rolled to a stop. A flickering neon sign declared The Liquor Box was open, though there were only two other vehicles in sight.

For several long minutes, he remained seated on his bike, feet planted on either side. Then, with a sense of inevitable doom, he dismounted and made his way into the bar that had witnessed the worst night of his life.

The large dining table in Penta's childhood home had chairs for eight. The two empty seats nagged her even as the bickering of her kids and the laughter of her father filled the room. Her mother's place was a bittersweet sorrow. But the one she'd reserved for Cash annoyed her.

She didn't know what she had to do to convince him he was a part of her family now. No matter what happened in the future, she hoped they'd remain friends. He didn't have to be alone anymore.

Even if he seemed to prefer it that way.

"Only one more year of university, hey, Felix?" Her father had picked up fried chicken tonight and he ladled gravy over his fries with a lavish hand. "Signed up for any interesting courses?"

Cyril ate with the single-minded intensity of a teenage boy. Abra and Delilah quarreled half-heartedly over who spent the most time in their shared bathroom. Penta focused on Felix.

He flicked an uneasy glance between his grandfather and his mother. "No, not yet."

Her back straightened in faint alarm. "What does that mean, not yet?"

He dragged the tines of his fork through the puddle of ketchup on his plate. "I've been offered a supervisor job."

"Good for you!" Pride didn't subdue the warning signals her radar was flashing. "But what does that have to do with school?"

"It's full-time. I can't keep up my course load and take the promotion."

Her father squinted. "You're not going back to school?"

"Of course he's going back." Penta's response was automatic. "Maybe they can adjust the job for you, make allowances for your classes."

"Maybe. But I didn't ask." Felix's chin rose and he finally met her gaze. "I don't want to go back to university. I've already accepted the promotion."

"Well, *un*accept it," she snapped. If only he'd talked to her first. She could have explained how she regretted not finishing her own degree so many years ago, stopped him from making the same mistake. "You can't quit now. You'll have wasted the last three years. How stupid can you be?"

The last words fell like ice shards into a ringing silence. Five pairs of eyes stared at her as if she'd grown horns. Aghast, she tried to backtrack. "I didn't mean it that way. I just—"

Felix regarded her with a sober expression. "It's my life, Mom. My decision. I start training on Monday. That's one of the reasons I can't go to Mexico with Dad. I'm sorry you're disappointed, but I'm not going back to school in September." Without giving her a chance to reply and with an air that declared he considered the subject closed, he turned to her father. "What do you think of the Jays chances at the pennant this year, Grampa?"

Jeremy shot her a quick sympathetic look before answering.

Penta could do nothing but sit, floundering in shock. She wanted to demand they discuss it further, wanted a chance to change his mind. Felix gave her no opportunity, ignoring her burning glares and moving the conversation along with mature determination. How could he be so calm when he was rejecting the plan they'd designed together? He'd been her rock since the divorce. Had she pushed him too hard? Was she the reason he was making this terrible mistake?

Cash hadn't been back to The Liquor Box at any time in the twelve years since his release. Hadn't expected he'd ever come back.

Wasn't sure why he had tonight.

The walls were a little dingier, the floor a little stickier, but the same cracked black vinyl stools ranged in front of the bar and the same hard metal chairs ringed wooden tables. Classic rock thundered from invisible speakers, pierced occasionally by raucous laughter and shouted expletives from the sparse Thursday evening crowd. Friday and Saturday had always been busier, when clean cut youths who lived outside the neighbourhood came looking for trouble, seeking to prove they were tough, not just privileged.

Men like the one who'd picked a fight with Cash all those years ago. His gaze shied away from the corner of the bar—*that* corner—remembering the dull clunk of skull hitting wood, the limp limbs slithering to the floor between one heartbeat and the next.

The bartender wasn't anyone he recognized—a hard, weary woman in a thin pink tank top and tight jeans. She looked forty and was probably not yet thirty. He ordered a bottle of beer—only idiots asked for a draft here—and when it came took a small wary sip.

"And who the fuck is this?" A vigorous slap on his shoulder shoved him forward, knocking his tooth against the bottle.

He twisted swiftly, planting his feet on the boot

rung of the stool, ready to launch himself into action—then juddered to a halt.

The grin on the other man's face was wide enough to reveal silver fillings on his molars. "Cash fuckin' Rylance. Couldn't believe it when you walked in. Just like fuckin' old times."

"Tyrone. Been a while." He slumped back on his stool and reached for his beer, hand unsteady after the adrenaline rush.

"Fuckin' right." Tyrone Jameson was a short squat man with dark hair, broad features, and a quick temper. They'd gone to high school together—when either of them bothered to go.

He hitched up onto the stool beside Cash, a dark glass bottle clenched in his fist. Always bulky, he'd gained a lot of weight over the years and his ass drooped over the edges. "How long you been out?" he asked in the casual tone of a man to whom jail was a simple fact of life.

Chapter Twenty-Three

"Twelve years." The weight of bad memories rooted Cash to the barstool.

"No shit. Time sure flies, huh?" Tyrone took a swig of his beer. "You still with Linda?"

A shiver of apprehension raced down his spine. He had no idea if Tyrone knew about Elle, but this was exactly what Linda had always worried about—his past tainting their daughter's future. "No."

Tyrone shrugged. "Way it goes, right?" and launched into a bitter recital of his most recent break up.

He let the words flow over him, grunting noncommittally, not really paying any attention, his mind swamped by unwelcome thoughts.

How odd that this grimy depressing place had been his refuge from the first time he'd snuck in at fifteen to that final disastrous night. The dim lighting did nothing to hide its beaten appearance, and the desperation of forlorn forgotten souls permeated the atmosphere. In the booth in the far corner, where he'd hung out with Tyrone and the others in his unofficial gang, a single man sat, twisting a tumbler in his hand, staring at the tabletop as if it held the answers to the universe. At another table, a man and woman argued with quiet ferocity, angry words camouflaged by the pounding music but unmistakable all the same.

He hated this place. Had hated it even then, just hadn't realized it. It represented everything terrible in his past, and he had to get out. Now.

He thunked his half-full bottle onto the bar. "I gotta go."

Tyrone blinked and then shrugged, expression flat. "Yeah, sure. See you around."

Cash hoped not. He really, really hoped not.

While he'd been inside, the sun had set. Dusk did its best to hide the garbage in the gutters, the grass poking up through the pavement, but couldn't disguise the scent of urine emanating from the narrow walkway beside the building.

Two young men stood next to his bike. One gripped the handlebars and swung a leg over the seat.

"Hey!" Cash lengthened his stride. "Get the hell off my bike!"

The men looked his way with identical sneers. "I'm not hurting it none," the sitting one said. "Relax, old man."

This was the tipping point on an already shitty day. Taut fiery emotions dredged up by revisiting the site of his biggest mistake, talking with an old friend, recalling the failures of his life, made the hair on his arms stand up and his nostrils flare. The familiar inclination to react first and deal with the consequences later swept over him. Time stood still as he battled to find the man he'd become, the man Penta believed in.

He clenched his fists and struggled to keep his voice to a growl, not a roar. "You don't touch a man's bike without asking first."

"You wasn't here to ask." The second young man touched the gleaming chrome fender with a reverent fingertip. "She's a beaut."

Cash's bunched muscles loosened a fraction at this sign of respect. "Yeah, she is. But this is not cool." He pointed a finger at the seated man. "Get off."

He took his time about it to show it was his decision, wasn't doing it because he'd been told. "We wasn't gonna steal it."

"Don't care. Take my advice. Don't touch a bike that's not your own ever again. The next guy might beat the crap out of you before you have a chance to explain."

"He could try." The reply was automatic, with no real heat behind it. He nudged his buddy with an elbow. "Beer's waiting." As one, they turned and headed into the bar.

Cash stood for another minute, letting his pulse settle. Then he climbed onto his bike and headed home, ready to put the past behind him for good.

Penta lay propped up on the pillows at the head of her bed and toyed with her phone. She desperately wanted to talk to someone about Felix's bombshell.

She could call Helen. The Silverberry matriarch would be sympathetic.

She could call her father. He might not be as understanding but would be honest.

She could call Cash. He'd tell her to let Felix make his own decisions, that it wasn't her place to command or compel her grown son. That wasn't what she wanted to hear, but it didn't matter. He was the one she wanted to tell her troubles to.

Her gaze slid to the empty side of the queen bed. He'd spent two nights there two weeks ago and his absence was almost as gaping as Mark's had been after twenty-two years of marriage. She reached for her phone.

He answered on the first ring, almost as if he'd been waiting. "Hey."

The single bass syllable resonated deep within her. She sighed in relief. "Hey."

"What's wrong?"

How did he know? What had he heard in her voice? "I'm sorry to call so late. Did I wake you?"

"No. You going to answer my question?"

She slid further down the pillows and rolled to her

side. Delilah and Abra would be asleep by now and there was little chance of disturbing them. Still, she kept the phone pressed to her ear and her voice low. "Felix isn't going back to university in the fall."

Cash's response was immediate. "And you think it's a mistake."

"Of course it's a mistake." Her whisper hissed with snake-like sibilance. "He only has one year left to finish his degree. Why not stick it out a little longer? Why throw away the last three years?"

He grunted, but she couldn't read the meaning behind it. "What's he going to do instead?"

"He's getting a promotion at work." Her free fingers pleated the cotton of her duvet cover.

"That's a good thing, isn't it?"

"Not at the expense of his education." There was no doubt in her mind about that. None at all.

Her flat, uncompromising statement severed the conversation like a machete. The longer the silence grew, the more restless and edgy she became. She broke first. "Cash?"

"I'm thinking. Wait." His tone brooked no disagreement.

She flopped onto her back, squiggled into a sitting position, reached for the velvet throw pillow she'd tossed aside when she'd climbed into bed an hour ago, and doodled in the plush nap.

His gravelly voice rumbled into her ear. "Are you upset because he's doing the same thing you did? Quitting university without a degree?"

She shouldn't have been surprised he remembered. Cash remembered everything. And the fact he could use that knowledge to pinpoint the deepest, darkest reason for her distress didn't shock her, either. She was beginning to think he knew her better than anyone ever had.

"Of course it is." Her own bitterness shocked her, but she kept on going. "How can I let Felix make the same mistake? All I'm asking for is one more year.

Then he can do whatever he wants. But at least he'd have that piece of paper to prove he'd done something with his life."

"Do you really define success by a piece of paper?" Cash's tone was sombre. "I didn't graduate high school, you know. I got my GED years later. And I learned mechanics on the job. I have no official accreditation."

Oh, god. She hadn't meant to make Cash feel as worthless as she felt herself. "You have something better. You have talent. I don't know much about motorcycles, but I know you have loyal customers because they trust your knowledge, your skills. You don't need a piece of paper to prove anything. To me or anyone else."

"Then why does Felix?"

Her mouth gaped open and closed like a beached fish. "That's different."

"Why?"

She had no answer. Tears of frustration burned her eyes.

"It's his decision, isn't it." It was a statement, not a question.

"Damn it." She held back a sob as her indignation deflated. "I suppose I have to let the girls go to Mexico too."

"You were always going to."

Again, his knowledge of her inner self was both flattering and irritating. She sighed. "Yeah."

"You're a good mom, Penta. You'll do what's right, even if it breaks your heart."

Letting her children stretch their wings and fly away might do that. "I want them to be happy."

"I know. But you can't define their happiness for them. You have to let them choose their paths."

"Like you did?" The words were out before she realized what a low blow they dealt. "I'm sorry, I didn't mean that the way it sounded. I know you've worked hard to improve your life, to recover from, well, everything. It's just"—she searched for words that didn't sound accusing—"don't you wish things had happened differently?"

"Every day, Penta. Every day."

Cash lay on his back, his phone flat on his chest in speaker mode, arms bent under his head, watching shadows and lights play across his ceiling.

"Do you think you and Linda would still be together if things hadn't happened the way they did?"

Penta's voice was so clear it was like she was lying next to him in the dimness. She'd never stayed the night, so he didn't have even that memory to warm his sheets. "I don't know. Probably not."

"Why?"

What he'd felt for Linda had been wan and weak compared to what he felt for Penta. Not that he was ready to put anything into words. He hadn't even said them out loud to himself. "Her father hated me, for one. He hated that his daughter was hanging around with a guy who grew up on the wrong side of town, worked with his hands. I think she was with me mostly to piss him off."

"That's kind of sad. For all of you." A transport truck rumbled by, the vibration rattling his bedroom window but not obscuring Penta's words. "I don't want my kids to feel trapped like that."

"Then you know what to do." He couldn't believe she had turned to him for parenting advice. Her trust warmed his chest.

"It's hard. The balance, I mean. Between letting them make their own mistakes and guiding them down the right path."

He could imagine. Linda had done a great job with Elle, as far as he could see, and he was just beginning to realize why she'd been so distraught when Elle had insisted on meeting him. She must have seen it as a rejection of the love she offered every day. A declaration that she wasn't enough.

A windy sigh gusted out of the speaker. "I guess I should let you go."

"No." He almost barked the word. "No," he repeated, softer. "I like talking to you like this."

"I like talking to you too." Her voice took on a teasing lilt. "Almost as much as I like kissing you."

His body reacted instantly. "Are you wearing those pajamas?"

The second night he'd stayed at her house, she'd come to bed swathed from chin to ankle in satiny pajamas decorated with teapots. He'd spent long sensual minutes dismantling the silken armor she'd donned, opening the shirt one button at a time, rubbing her core through the slippery fabric, using her shields against her until she'd been moaning and begging.

"Maybe. What about you?"

"You know I sleep naked." He smiled at her hiss of appreciation. "Ever had phone sex?"

"Nuh-uh."

Her wordless response played a melody of arousal, of need, of curiosity. He unwound one arm from behind his head and slid his hand under the blanket to grip his cock. "Are you touching yourself, Penta?"

A gasp was her only answer.

"What a bad girl." He knew that's what she wanted to hear. In reality, she was too good for words. Definitely too good for him. Though he was beginning to hope he might deserve her someday. "Now, here's what I want you to do."

Chapter Twenty-Four

Cash knew he shouldn't let his guard down. Fate revelled in screwing him over when things were going well.

True summer temperatures had waited until mid-July to blaze down on Prince George. His shop had no air-conditioning and keeping all the doors open didn't produce enough of a cross draft to help. His apartment was worse. Not that he was spending much time there.

No, he was spending most of his non-working hours at Penta's. The last two weeks had been two of the best of his life. Her older children no longer regarded him with open suspicion and Abra accepted him with the innocence of a well-loved child. Penta's shyness and his own reluctance to have sex with her kids in the house had evaporated and he'd slept over several nights.

The first hint that life was about to kick him in the balls occurred the afternoon of the last Wednesday of the month.

He was closing the shop early in order to take Elle and Cyril to a nearby lake, everyone in search of a respite from the scorching heat. The two were thick as thieves now that Cyril had worked off his sentence. Linda and Penta seemed to have no trouble with the friendship, but Cash had mixed feelings. He'd decided being their chauffeur whenever possible was the subtlest way to keep an eye on them.

Giving the nearly complete Baby Bonnie a pat, he

began tidying his workspace so it would be ready when he returned.

And that was when Tyrone Jameson strolled through the front door.

"Cash, my man!" He sauntered over, his huge belly and bulging thighs draped ironically in a Toronto Raptors basketball jersey and athletic shorts. Damp patches on his chest and under his arms darkened the shiny fabric. "Been thinking about you since seeing you in the bar. Wanted to check out your digs."

Cash wiped sweat from his forehead and upper lip with a mostly clean rag. He deeply regretted the impulse that had drawn him to The Liquor Box and had no intention of renewing an acquaintance with Tyrone or anyone from the bad old days.

And he did *not* want Tyrone to meet Elle or Cyril. Both of whom would be here any minute.

"Sorry. You picked a bad time. I'm closing up early today. Was just about to lock up." Laying a heavy hand on Tyrone's shoulder, he attempted to propel him back to the door, ignoring the unpleasantly moist skin under his palm.

Tyrone didn't so much as shift his weight. His smile glittered with a wicked edge. "What? Don't have ten fuckin' minutes for an old friend? You blew me off at the bar too."

"Didn't blow you off then and not blowing you off now." A lie, of course. But Tyrone could make a bad enemy if he knew the truth. "I just got places to be."

"I told Jordy I ran into you."

Cash dropped his hand like he'd been shocked by a faulty ignition cable. "Why the fuck you do that?" He was being sucked back into the life he'd avoided for twelve lonely years. Even his grammar was devolving to his pre-prison, non-reading days.

Jordy had been at The Liquor Box the night Cash had almost taken a man's life. The night he had destroyed his own. In fact, Jordy had been the one to egg him on, to toss down the gauntlet by calling Cash a coward if he didn't stand up for himself over the grievous insult of being bumped into in a busy bar.

It sounded so stupid now. *Was* stupid.

Tyrone watched him with smug insolence. "He runs the gang. Lots of guys with bikes in it. Figured you could use the business."

No. It was a silent cry of rage. "Thanks for the thought, but I'm pretty busy. Don't know if I could take on much more." Jordy was probably looking for a tame mechanic who would turn a blind eye to any illegalities. He *couldn't* return to that world. Losing Elle now he'd finally found her would shred his soul. And the look of disappointment on Penta's face would be unbearable.

"Oh, I'm thinking you can." Tyrone's threatening tone was impossible to miss.

Why had he sought him out now? Cash wasn't hard to find. He had a website, for Christ's sake. It could only be because of Cash's idiotic action in going back to The Liquor Box.

He had to get Tyrone out. Now. He gripped a fat, flabby bicep and took another step toward the door. Tyrone resisted, his sheer bulk making him difficult to budge.

It was too late. Elle and Cyril entered, giggling and grinning, and stopped short when they caught sight of the two men.

"What's going on, Dad?" Elle's smile faltered, her gaze flicking from one to the other.

Cyril stepped in front of her, his scrawny fists clenching, but said nothing. The boy was developing excellent instincts.

Cash let go of Tyrone but remained at his elbow. If two self-absorbed teenagers had known instantly something was wrong, the atmosphere was more strained than he realized. "Nothing."

Tyrone raised an eyebrow at him. "Dad?"

With the click of gears engaging, he realized the damage had been done. He'd grown so used to Elle using the word he hadn't even heard it this time. His level of alert flared into the red zone.

He looked at Cyril and jerked his chin. "You two go wait in the back. This guy was just leaving."

"This guy?" Tyrone stepped forward and held out a meaty hand. "I'm Tyrone. Your *dad* and I were best friends growing up."

"Really?" Elle's expression brightened, her curiosity piqued.

Tyrone turned to Cyril. "And who are you?"

Cyril shook the offered hand warily. "Cyril Potter."

"You look familiar. You know my son TJ?"

Cyril's eyes widened and he slid a guilty glance at Cash. "TJ Jameson? Yeah, I guess."

Tyrone laughed and slapped Cyril on the shoulder, causing him to stumble forward. "Thought I'd seen you around. One of my boy's buds, hey?"

The web had tangled even further. "Elle. Cyril." Cash knew his tone was harsh, but he had to get them away. "Back room. Now."

Cyril took Elle's hand and dragged her past. She protested, but Cyril shot half-frightened looks over his shoulder as he hustled her down the hall.

Tyrone followed their departure with a speculative eye. "Pretty girl."

White-hot fury burned from Cash's gut to every nerve ending. "Stay away from her."

"I'd be more worried about that boy she's with. If he's who I think he is, he's a pussy. TJ needed to teach some fucker a lesson and he refused."

Cool relief flooded Cash at this news. He had wondered but hadn't wanted to ask Cyril. Then the second penny dropped. "Your son wrecked my shop."

Tyrone frowned and looked around. "Seems okay to me."

"Couple months ago. Some assholes smashed all the glass, tried to break into my cash drawer, vandalized the place. I caught one of them." He pointed toward the back. "Cyril. He's spent the last weeks working off the damage your son and his gang did. And not once did he give up his buddies, not even when I threatened to take him to the cops."

Tyrone shrugged. "Maybe he's not as spineless as TJ thinks."

No word of apology for what his son had done. Not even an acknowledgment it had happened. Cash's breath hissed in and out as he struggled to control his outrage.

He took one long stride forward and came nose to nose with Tyrone. "Get out of my shop. Don't come back. Tell Jordy thanks but no thanks."

Tyrone glared, black eyes sunken in the flesh of his round face. Cash prayed this visit hadn't been suggested by Jordy. The other man had much less at stake if he were just trying to curry the leader's favour, not following orders.

After several tense seconds, Tyrone's sullen scowl melted into false bonhomie. "Hey, man, it's all good. Just trying to do you a solid. You don't want me to put a word in, I won't."

Cash didn't unfurl his fists until his so-called friend was out of sight.

The sky was beginning to pinken. Abra and Delilah stood at the living room window, noses pressed against the glass, waiting with fizzing anticipation for Mark, Jacinta, and her two sons to arrive. Two suitcases and two carry-on bags waited by the front door.

Penta's heart was breaking.

"You going to make it?" Cash wrapped his arms around her from behind and rested his chin on her head.

Afraid she'd start weeping if she unclamped her lips, she nodded and leaned back against his sturdy warmth. Last night had been the first time he'd stayed over without a direct invitation. He'd known in his

Cash-like way that she would need his support this morning.

She'd wanted to go to the airport to see everyone off, eager to extend the final minutes with her daughters. Mark had quashed that. "You'll make a scene, and everyone will be crying before we get through security. If the girls get homesick, I'd like to put it off until we are in Mexico at least."

She sniffed back tears, hating to admit he had a point.

Cyril and Felix slouched up from the basement, yawning and bleary-eyed at the 4:30 a.m. wake up call.

"Have fun, squirts." Felix ruffled Abra's hair but knew better than to touch Delilah's short yet carefully arranged strands.

The atmosphere between Penta and her eldest son was still strained. It didn't help that he was revelling in his new work responsibilities. She was certain not returning to university was a huge mistake, but each day he grew in confidence and maturity. Her influence had slipped away without her noticing. When he'd been a child, she could win an argument with "because I said so." Not anymore.

Cyril mumbled something to his sisters and then fell into an upholstered chair and closed his eyes. He, too, was rarely home these days. He was spending a lot of time with Elle and as much as she liked the girl, she couldn't help but worry. She'd had the safe sex talk with him for the second time, which he'd listened to with burning ears and averted eyes, all while saying it wasn't like that. She didn't believe him.

The Airporter transfer van Mark had hired rolled into the driveway. Abra raced to open the door, waving madly before turning back for her luggage, and Delilah swung her backpack onto one shoulder.

Be good." Penta hugged her so tight she squirmed. "I love you. Take care of your sister."

"I will. Bye, Mom. See you in a month." She

vanished outside.

Penta helped Abra straighten the straps of her own backpack, noting the fragility of her shoulders, the delicate stalk of her neck. Her baby was leaving her, and she would miss the last month of her childhood. When she returned, she would be in high school. Everything would be different then.

Everything was already different.

She embraced her, laying her cheek on the soft curly hair and giving into tears, speaking between sobs. "I love you so much. I'm going to miss you."

"Don't cry, Mommy." Abra's voice quivered, and when she pulled away her own eyes brimmed. "Don't cry."

"I'm not. I won't." She sniffled fiercely. A large warm hand landed on her back, and she drew strength from Cash's silent presence. "Have a good time. Use your journal so you can tell me everything when you get back."

"I will." Still, Abra didn't move.

"What's the hold up?" Mark appeared in the doorway.

His frown of disapproval raked Penta's already frayed nerves. All she could do was shake her head.

Though his mouth tightened at the sheen of tears in Abra's eyes, he was smart enough not to comment. "Let's go, honey. Everyone's waiting for you." He held the door wide as she bumped her suitcase through, looking over her shoulder with trembling lips.

Penta followed, drawn by the irresistible magnet of motherhood. "You're going to have a great time, baby." She made a shooing gesture. "Go on now."

Her daughter straggled down the sidewalk, handed her luggage to the van driver, and climbed in.

Penta gripped Mark's arm. "You'll take care of them, right? Make sure they message me as soon as you arrive."

His stern expression softened. "I will. Thanks for letting them come, Penta." He looked past her and she followed his gaze to Cash. The men nodded, and she had the distinct feeling the responsibility for her well-being had been officially transferred. She should have been insulted but didn't have the energy.

Before she knew it, her driveway was as empty as her heart. Cyril and Felix drifted downstairs to snatch some more sleep before the day truly began. Cash took her limp hand and drew her to the large, upholstered chair Cyril had vacated. He sat down, tugged her onto his lap, and held her as she sobbed.

Chapter Twenty-Five

Penta was well-accustomed to the "absent child" phenomenon. When even just one of her children was away from home, their lack created an emptiness that outweighed all else. With both her daughters gone, half her life was sucked out. As for Felix and Cyril, they might as well have been ghosts, the first busy with his new job and the second with Elle.

Being with Cash helped. He introduced her to a few of his favourite authors and they had wonderful arguments about what they liked and didn't like to read. Long sunny evenings gave them plenty of time to ride after he finished work. And when he confessed he loved her baking but did little himself, she spent a pleasant afternoon creating a recipe book filled with her favourites—for which he thanked her in delightful ways.

Still, she had far too many empty hours to fill. She should have used them to find a job. But her enthusiasm for that project had vanished.

Cash's insightful comments had forced her to examine her reaction to Felix's rejection of university. Yes, she was disappointed. Yes, she wished he'd made a different decision. But her anger and the way she'd lashed out came from an unexpected source.

Jealousy.

It was humiliating to admit, but there it was. Felix had been living the life she'd exchanged for motherhood, the life she'd never had but missed with an unexpected ache. While she'd never regret giving her children the attention they deserved, maybe she regretted not finding a better balance between her own needs and theirs.

Feeling as if prying eyes were boring into her back, she explored the local university's website. She wondered if the credits she'd received almost two decades ago would still be valid. Not that she could go back to school at her age. It would be degrading, sitting in a classroom with fresh-faced teenagers. This was just a distraction, something to keep her mind off her girls.

Eight days after they left, she stood in the kitchen waiting for her morning coffee to perk. Her gaze fell on the calendar tacked to the bulletin board. In the past, the squares had been filled with the numerous activities and appointments a large family generated. This month, it was shockingly blank.

The British Columbia Day long weekend stretched ahead, and an impulsive idea seized her. She grabbed her phone and started to search. The chances of finding a cabin available at such short notice on the busiest weekend of the year were infinitesimal, but it didn't hurt to try.

Cash pulled into Penta's driveway, still chewing on the mysterious text she'd sent three hours ago.

I hope you don't have plans for this weekend. Pack for three nights. Bring a swimsuit—or not. Can we take the bike?

Of course he didn't have plans. Any that didn't involve her, at least. And take the bike where? Not that it mattered. He'd go anywhere with Penta.

He was relieved she sounded like herself again. She'd taken the girls' absence hard—far harder than he'd liked. But this message brimmed with sweet energy and teasing optimism. Maybe Penta Unleashed was back.

His feet had barely hit the concrete when she popped out of the front door, a backpack on her shoulders, two carrier bags dangling from one hand, and his spare helmet—*her* helmet—from the other. She kept it at her place now. It had seemed silly to continue packing it back and forth when she was the only one who used it.

"Hi." She pecked him on the cheek, angling her head to avoid his helmet. "Ready?"

"Ready for what, exactly?"

Her cheeks were flushed, eyes bright, grin so wide her lids crinkled. "I booked us a cabin at Vivian Lake. I need to get out of the house. I never thought I'd find something so late, not for a long weekend, but they had a last-minute cancellation."

"Just you and me?" He would never begrudge Penta's focus on her family. It was one of the things he lov...*liked* about her. He'd hoped to have her all to himself someday but hadn't expected her to suggest it.

"Yes. Felix and Cyril will be fine. It'll be good practice for when they move out." Her voice cracked a little on the last words, yet her grin never wavered. "We'll still be in cell range. If they need anything, they can call."

Overwhelmed with tenderness, he dismounted, cupped her face in his palms and kissed her. She leaned into the caress, her mouth opening, tongue tangling. Pride swelled that she'd chosen *him* to be her lover, her friend.

She broke the connection, sinking back onto her heels and lifting the carrier bags still twisted round her fingers. "Help me with these?"

He brushed her lips with his thumb and her eyes darkened. "Of course." He spied soft drinks, a bottle of wine, bagels, hot dogs, and several bell peppers among other items as he loaded the saddlebags.

"I thought we could stop and pick up a couple steaks on our way out of town. Or anything else you might want that we can fit onto the bike. The cabin has the basic condiments, and there's a small store on-site." Penta strapped on her helmet and tucked the curly strands of her shiny brown hair underneath. She hadn't cut it since he'd known her, and ringlets bounced on the back of her neck.

"Steak sounds great." It did, but that wasn't what had his juices flowing. The thought of being alone with Penta for three nights and two days, without the distraction of children or old enemies or ex-partners was what set his appetite roaring. He settled into the driver's position, and she swung a leg over the pillion seat, shuffling into place, her familiar softness amping up his heightened senses. "Ready?"

She nodded, her helmet bumping his gently. "I am. Let's ride!"

Her attempts at biker slang never failed to amuse him, and he laughed out loud as he rolled onto the street.

An entire weekend. Just him and Penta. He gunned the engine and sent them flying.

Penta woke to the whisper of a calloused hand caressing her body. The faint scent of pine drifted in the open window, mingling with Cash's earthy aroma. She hummed in contentment.

Her eyes drifted open as she shifted toward his warm naked bulk, her feet tangling in the sheets crumpled at the bottom of the bed. The tiny one-room cabin was stifling, even though the sun had gone down hours ago, the heated air heavy as a blanket.

His jutting brows shadowed his eyes, while light from the almost full moon glinted off the silvery strands in his beard. Her breath caught as his fingers sought her breast, thumb straying over her rising nipple.

"What time is it?" she murmured. They'd barely made it in the door before falling into bed and had climbed out only long enough to share a supper of premade grocery-store salad, the high temperatures discouraging them from lighting the barbeque.

"Not quite two." He lowered his head to nip her collarbone, beard rough against her skin.

A stirring near her hip enticed her to wriggle closer. "Again?"

"Always." His roving hand stilled an instant before floating lower. "Besides, I might never get you all to myself like this ever again."

Blunt fingertips stroked her core and rational thought fled. Blindly, she reached between them and grasped his cock, working him up and down, matching the rhythm of his pulsing invasion. His breath hissed in and out. Her heart rate soared. He leaned over and took her mouth, pressing kiss upon kiss on her lips, muttering words of encouragement, praise, and lust, driving her closer to the edge...

His cell phone rang.

They froze like teenagers caught in the act. Penta stared, panting and wide-eyed. Cash's face went blank.

It rang again. He flung himself off the bed and scrambled for his pants.

Nothing good ever came from a phone call in the wee hours. She'd written Cash's number on the instructions she'd left for the boys. If something had happened, would they call him instead of breaking the bad news to her directly?

Nightmare scenarios raced through her mind. The world was a dangerous place. How could she have left them to fend for themselves?

After what seemed an eon, each shrill chime piercing her soul, Cash finally found the phone. It took him three swipes and several curses to connect the call. "Elle? What's wrong?"

Not her boys. Her children were safe. Her cheeks prickled with goosebumps as the adrenaline subsided from her system.

"Calm down, sweetheart. I can't understand you."

The knobs on Cash's spine stood out sharp and taut under his skin as he hunched over, the phone clenched in his fist. In the darkness, the colourful design on his left shoulder blade was nothing but black swirls. "Where are you now? Okay, good. Have you called your mother?"

Remorse engulfed her. Her children might be okay, but Cash's only daughter obviously wasn't. Inaudible, agitated squawks leaked from the speaker, but she couldn't decipher any words.

"I'll be there as soon as I can, all right? But I'm not at home. It will take me about forty-five minutes." Another pause, more desperate sounds from the phone. "I'm sorry. I'm leaving right away. I'll call you once I'm on my bike. We'll stay in touch the entire time. I promise. Just give me two minutes to get dressed."

By now, Penta was out of bed and wriggling into her leggings. After a few more hurried, placating words to Elle, Cash tossed the phone aside and dragged on his jeans and T-shirt.

"What happened?" Penta gave up the search for her bra and tugged her sweatshirt on. "Is she okay?"

"No, she's not okay." He stomped into his boots and knelt to tie the laces with sharp jerks. "Not fucking okay at all."

His savage tone caused her to fumble as she reached for her own boots, and the violent glare in his eyes made her fingers nerveless.

"Cyril took her to a house party at goddamn TJ Jameson's place and proceeded to get roaring drunk. When Elle tried to leave, TJ and his asshole friends blocked her way. She's locked herself in the bathroom, too terrified to come out."

"Cyril? Drunk?" Stunned, Penta groped for her bootlaces without tearing her gaze from Cash's hard, brutal expression. "Why would he go to a party at TJ's? He doesn't hang out with those horrible boys anymore."

"Are you sure about that?" He snatched his keys off the floor where they'd fallen out of his pants.

Her skin went cold. "What do you mean?"

"I don't have time to explain. My daughter had to barricade herself in a fucking toilet to avoid getting assaulted. Because of *your* son." He strode out of the cabin. She scrambled after him, hopping on one foot.

"Cash! Wait!" She shoved her second boot on, not bothering with the laces. The engine thundered into life, and she clambered onto the passenger seat. Before she had a chance to grab hold, he was off.

Chapter Twenty-Six

Cash was aware of little more than his daughter's voice in his ear as he ignored speed limits and stop signs on his way to her side.

But he couldn't ignore the sickening stew of self-hate bubbling in his gut.

He shuddered each time Penta's body brushed his as the bike swayed around corners and accelerated on the infrequent straight stretches. Her stupid, stupid son had put his daughter in danger. Though it was ultimately Cash's fault, he had more than enough rage to go around.

Penta, for being too lenient as a parent.

Cyril, for bringing Elle to the party.

Tyrone, for masterminding the plan. Because Cash had no doubt this was a twisted punishment for rejecting the gang's business.

The neighbourhood where Tyrone lived—the neighbourhood Cash had escaped—was frequently patrolled by cops. He couldn't afford to be stopped for a traffic violation, not now, not in this mood, so gritted his teeth with bitter impatience as he negotiated the streets with care.

"Almost there, baby." Elle's distraught directions had been vague and incomplete, but she'd managed to landmark the house within a block or two. He could only hope to find signs of the party. In this area, the neighbours didn't call the authorities if the music was too loud or a fight broke out on someone's front lawn.

"There." Penta pointed over his shoulder. She hadn't said a word the entire ride. "Felix's car. Maybe he came to get Cyril. God, I hope everyone's okay."

At the moment, he couldn't give two fucks about Penta's sons. He'd come for Elle and Elle alone. Steering the bike onto the buckled sidewalk, he killed the engine. The thump of drums and scream of guitars bled from a house two doors down. "I'm here, Elle. Stay in the bathroom. I'll be right there."

Penta slid off the seat. She hadn't wrapped her arms around him as she always did when they rode and had used his shoulders as a prop only when necessary. He'd been torn between needing her familiar embrace and relief that she hadn't touched him except when unavoidable.

His focus was on Elle—*had* to be on Elle—yet curdling underneath that grinding anxiety was the realization his time with Penta was finished. When she found out this debacle was his fault it would all be over. His heart cracked into a thousand shards of glass.

Tearing off his helmet, he tossed it to the ground. Penta was on his heels as he stormed up the dilapidated wooden steps leading to the open front door. The music rattled his teeth, and the stench of weed choked his nostrils. Without sparing a glance for the bodies sprawled on the floor and furniture of the front room, he headed down the short hallway to his right. Three closed doors greeted him.

"Elle?" He tried the handle of the first. It opened and he caught sight of pumping buttocks and chunky legs pointing at the ceiling.

A girl with blue eyeshadow looked over a tattooed shoulder and shrieked. "Get out. Get out!"

He slammed the door shut and tried the one on the other side of the hall. Locked. "Elle? It's Dad. Are you in there?"

The knob wriggled and he released it. The door opened and he glimpsed a mascara-streaked, tear-stained face before Elle fell into his arms. "Oh, Daddy! I was so scared!"

"I know, honey. I know." He stroked her long, dishevelled hair with a shaking hand. "Let's get you out of here."

Tucking her to his side, he led her to the front room. Empty liquor bottles covered every flat surface, and the air was grimy with smoke. As they passed the couch, a young man with the same heavy-set build, dark hair, and broad face as Tyrone rolled his neck and peered up at them. With the laziness of the very drunk and totally stoned, he smirked at Cash. "She's kinda young for you, ain't she? And she's a cold bitch. Wouldn't play when we wanted to."

The marrow in his bones flowed like molten lava, yet he continued toward the front door, determined to get Elle away from this hellhole.

Until the raucous rock assaulting his ears cut off abruptly and a voice stopped him.

"Is that any way to speak to Elle's daddy, TJ?"

A chorus of mumbled protests from the more lucid partiers filled the void left by the music. Cash turned, pushing Elle behind him but keeping a hold of her hand. "You. You set this up."

Tyrone stood in the opening leading to a cluttered, filthy kitchen. He placed the wireless speaker he'd apparently just turned off on the counter, crossed his arms over his bulbous belly, and slouched negligently against the wall. "All I did was suggest TJ have some buds over. Your girl and her pansy friend could have said no. The rest...just happened."

Berserk fury swamped him. He grabbed the asshole by the front of his shirt and smashed his fist into the leering face. Tyrone shouted, blood pouring from his nose, and swung a wild overhand that connected viciously with the side of Cash's head. His ears rang and eyes watered, but his grip on Tyrone's damp shirt didn't slip. He jabbed, quick and fierce and powerful, knuckles sinking deep into a soft flabby gut.

Tyrone doubled over on a sharp gasp and Cash let him drop to the floor.

With shining crystal clarity, he knew he was going to kill the bastard. Knew he would gladly go to jail for the rest of his life to protect his daughter. He drew back his foot, clad in its heavy motorcycle boot.

"Cash! No!" Penta stepped between them.

"Get out of my way." He could have lifted her to the side, but didn't want to stain her with the hands that had punished Tyrone.

"I won't. I won't let you do this." She pressed her palm to his chest. At her feet, Tyrone rolled to his side, retched, and vomited. She didn't budge.

"He planned this. Hoping someone would hurt Elle. Because of me."

"Don't do this. Not here. Not now."

A muscle juddered at the corner of his eye so hard Penta flickered like a mirage on the horizon. Of course she didn't want him to beat the crap out of the piece of shit. She would rather speak sternly, maybe take away his cell phone privileges as if he were a teenager, not a grown man who had known exactly what he was doing.

Elle appeared at his elbow. Her lips trembled. "Please, Dad. Let's go. Please."

Her terrified gaze bore into him. The red haze obscuring his vision receded. What had he been thinking? She'd been through enough tonight, without having to watch her father brawling.

Moving with stiff heaviness, he took Elle's hand once more and tugged her out the door. He didn't look back, but sensed Penta following.

He wasn't surprised to see Cyril huddled on the curb at the end of the walk, head in his hands. Penta wouldn't have left that house without him. Still struggling to regain his sanity, he halted on the sidewalk.

Penta bent down and picked up their helmets, lying discarded on the hard-packed grass of the front lawn. "Cyril took Felix's car. Without permission and illegally, since he hasn't passed his Novice test yet. I'm going to drive him home. Are you okay taking Elle on the bike?"

He absorbed her words sluggishly. The last time he'd felt so detached from reality was standing in the courtroom hearing his sentence decided. "Yeah."

"I want to go home, Dad." Despite the warmth of the night, Elle vibrated with shivers. She wore only a thin tank and denim shorts that barely reached her thighs, so Cash shrugged out of his sweatshirt and dropped it over her, leaving himself bare-chested.

Penta offered her helmet to Elle, then held out his. Cash accepted it, careful not to touch her. She prodded Cyril with her foot. "Let's go. If you throw up in the car, you'll be cleaning it the minute we get home. I don't care how awful you feel."

The boy rose with careful movements, wobbly and weak. Once on his feet, he spared Cash a miserable glance. "I'm sorry. It's all my fault."

Penta motioned toward the car. "We'll talk about it later, when everyone is calmer."

"I want to go home. I need to go home." Elle's high falsetto revealed she was at the end of her endurance.

"We're going." He led her toward his bike. Penta and Cyril went in the opposite direction.

He'd always known his time with Penta would end, had wondered what the final straw would be. This was worse than anything he'd ever imagined.

And nothing more than he deserved.

Chapter Twenty-Seven

As Penta pulled away, Cyril rolled down his window and stuck his head out.

"If you're going to be sick, tell me and I'll pull over. Otherwise, it will just end up splattered down the side."

He made a pained gurgling noise and waved a limp hand.

She had so many questions she didn't know where to start. But they would have to wait. Cyril was in no shape to explain what had happened.

She couldn't blame Cash for his violence. She'd come back from ushering Cyril outside in time to hear TJ and Tyrone's inflammatory words. Primitive satisfaction had sung in her veins when Cash's blow had drawn blood.

But she couldn't stand by and let him destroy everything he'd worked so hard to build in the last twelve years. That was why she'd prevented him from delivering savage justice. It had been for his sake, no one else's.

Nonetheless, his brutality worried her. She had never seen him lost to rage. When she'd looked into his eyes, her hand pressed to his chest, she hadn't seen Cash—the wistful loner, the giving lover, the skilled craftsman, the avid reader. She'd seen a pitiless stranger.

Cyril made it home without vomiting, but the moment he staggered into the house he made a beeline for the nearest bathroom. Seconds later, harsh retching sounded loud and clear through the closed door. She retraced her steps to the garage and retrieved two cans of ginger ale from the second fridge there.

She waited for Cyril's purging to end and then helped him down the stairs and into bed. Opening one can, she handed it to him and placed the other on his nightstand.

"Drink this. It'll help." She brushed his hair off his damp temples, studying his greenish pallor. "Did you do any drugs, Cyril?" If he had, should she take him to the hospital? What if he'd taken something laced with fentanyl?

"Just booze." He mumbled the words, eyes closed tightly, lips creased. "Wouldn't smoke. Wouldn't do pills. Told 'em I wouldn't. 'S why I had to drink."

"What do you mean, had to?"

"Said did shots...leave Elle alone. Didn't want...hurt her. 'S my fault. All my fault."

Penta frowned. Was there more behind tonight than youthful idiocy? Cash had also said something similar, taking the blame on his shoulders. What was she missing?

Cyril fell into a restless doze. She made sure a bucket was nearby and tucked him in. Instead of going up two flights to her own bed, she collapsed onto the couch in the rec room just outside Cyril and Felix's bedrooms. Dragging an ancient, holey, crocheted blanket off the back, she let exhaustion take her.

The next she knew, Felix was shaking her awake. "Mom? What are you doing down here?"

"Cyril." She struggled to a sitting position. "Can you check him?"

Forehead creased, Felix disappeared into his brother's room and reappeared shortly. "What's wrong with him? He's asleep but doesn't look too good. And it stinks in there."

"He's drunk." She yawned and scrubbed her

cheeks. "What time is it?"

"Seven. I have to be at work soon. What do you mean, drunk?"

God. She'd barely had three hours sleep. Gone were the days when she could function after disrupted nights. "Where were you last night? Didn't you hear him take your car?"

"He took my car?" Felix's voice rose out of his cautious whisper, loud with annoyance. "I was out with Hadiyyah. She drove me home about midnight and I came in the front door instead of the garage. What was he thinking?"

Penta made a mental note to ask who Hadiyyah was later. For now, her focus had to be Cyril. "I don't imagine he was thinking in general." She swung her feet to the floor, back aching, and shoved to her feet. "Come on. I'll explain everything over a cup of coffee."

Felix's expression swung from alarm to anger to anxiety as she related the events between sips of caffeine. "You're right. He really wasn't thinking," he agreed when she got to the end of her tale. "I never thought he'd be so stupid. His door was closed when I went down. I should have checked he was there. Maybe if I had, we could have found them sooner."

"It's not your fault. I don't expect you to keep tabs on him."

"That's exactly what you asked me to do."

He was right. She had, shortly after Cash had apprehended Cyril. "That was a short-term thing. It's my job. I'm the one who should have been here last night." Instead of having bone-melting sex with Cash. The guilt she'd buried under concern for Cyril broke free. Acid churned in her empty stomach.

"Or maybe Cyril shouldn't have been an idiot and just stayed home." Felix threw his last bit of toast into his mouth and drained his milk. "I have to go."

"Are you really not going back to university?" Sleep deprivation must have lowered her inhibitions. The words escaped her without conscious thought.

Felix paused in the doorway. "Mom—" His tone held warning and frustration in equal measure.

Still, she couldn't let it go. "Hear me out. Just for a second." She drew in a deep breath. "You know I went to university, right?"

"Yeah." His expression remained guarded, but at least he was listening.

"I know I did the right thing, quitting school to take care of my family. But that doesn't mean I don't regret it. I don't want you to feel the same way."

He shook his head, mouth pressed tight. "If someday I do, you can say I told you so. I'm sorry to disappoint you, but I'm not going to change my mind. I like my job, and they're already talking about giving me more responsibility."

"You are so close. What's one more year?" She had to make him understand. He couldn't make the same mistake she had.

"I'm not going back, Mom. Stop asking me." The door closed quietly behind him, followed by the hum of the garage opener.

Cash's irregular hours never bothered his customers, as long as he posted the changes on his website and made sure the message on his business line was current. Since he'd already announced he'd be closed for the long weekend, he didn't bother opening on Saturday.

He wondered about the cabin. Someone would have to get the groceries and clothes and bathroom items they'd abandoned in their haste. He should probably discuss that with Penta, but didn't have the nerve to call her. Not yet.

Thinking these random thoughts didn't keep the memories of last night at bay. He was consumed by them.

Too restless to stay in his apartment, he went downstairs, though working on the Bonnie in his current haphazard state of mind was out of the question. Any joy he'd taken in restoring the Tiger Cub had been sapped. He ended up sitting listlessly on his work stool, staring into space and rubbing the knuckles of his right hand, which still ached from their contact with Tyrone's face.

He didn't regret the punches he'd thrown. Not one bit. But he deeply regretted Elle had seen them.

She had clung to him with panicky strength as he'd driven her slowly and carefully home. Every once in a while, she shuddered and warm wet tears slid down his bare back.

He'd called Linda before they left Tyrone's, giving her the gist of what had happened. She was standing at the front door when they arrived. Open housecoat flapping like wings, she flew down the step and hugged Elle before she had a chance to dismount. Their daughter's sobbing intensified, and Linda stared frantically at Cash.

"She says she's not hurt." He widened his stance and planted his feet so the women's combined weight wouldn't topple the bike.

Linda's gaze flickered between them. "Why did she call you? Why not me?"

He had wondered the same thing. "You'll have to ask her."

"Come on, sweetheart." Linda urged her off the bike. "What were you thinking, sneaking out of the house?"

"I'm sorry. I'm so sorry. You must be so mad at me." Elle's wail of despair echoed down the dawn-still street.

A dog barked and a light went on in the closest house. He didn't want this homecoming to be fodder for gossip. "Go inside with your mom, honey." He pressed a hand on Elle's shoulder.

Linda had ushered her to the door without further questions, pausing only to toss a warning to Cash over her shoulder as they went. "We're going to talk about this later. Don't think we aren't."

Which was probably why he was so edgy. He was not looking forward to that discussion. He'd have to confess exactly why Elle had been in such danger, and it would only reinforce what Linda had believed all these years. No way would she let him near Elle again, not after this.

It didn't matter that he deserved the sentence, just as he'd deserved to go to jail. Knowing you earned your punishment didn't make it any easier to take.

Chapter Twenty-Eight

He didn't hear from either Penta or Linda all day Saturday. He assumed they were so furious they couldn't bear talking to him. And who could blame them?

He certainly didn't.

By Sunday afternoon, his apartment was the cleanest it had ever been, and the stockroom alphabetized. He'd even been to a nearby gym, paid a drop-in fee, and done weight work until his muscles screamed from the unaccustomed exercise.

Popping a couple Advil might alleviate the pain, but he didn't, hoping the discomfort in his body might distract him—at least temporarily—from his mental misery.

His phone buzzed with a text as he stared dully into his fridge, wondering what might tempt his non-existent appetite. He closed the appliance door carefully and regarded the cell lying on the counter with apprehension. As much as he longed to hear from any of the women in his life, he wasn't looking forward to it.

The screen went black before he could read who had messaged him. Cautiously, as if the device were a bomb, he tapped it awake.

Penta. *Do you have time to talk?*

The rage and fury he'd felt toward Cyril, and to a lesser extent Penta, had long since faded. He recognized now he had been trying to spread the blame when it rested on his shoulders alone. If he hadn't gone back to his old haunts, if he hadn't refused Tyrone's so-called offer of gang business, if he hadn't been the man he was, everything would be as it had been Friday.

He'd still have Penta. He'd still have Elle. He'd still have a family.

With doomed resignation, he typed *Yes*.

The dots danced immediately. *I'll be there in fifteen minutes.*

Of course she wanted to speak face to face. Penta wasn't the kind of person who broke up with someone over the phone.

Well, he wasn't a coward, either. When she made the break, he'd accept it with grace, instead of falling on his knees and pleading for another chance. She deserved someone...cleaner. Someone untainted. Someone as bright and life-affirming as herself.

Anyone other than him.

Penta stumbled up the stairs to Cash's apartment. She'd gone to the cabin to retrieve their belongings, and the bag stuffed with his things banged against her knees.

That discomfort was nothing compared to the trepidation tripping in her heart.

He'd been so angry when they'd rescued Cyril and Elle. And he'd had a right to be. Her son had taken his daughter into danger, and though she now knew the reasons why, that didn't make it all better.

She only hoped Cash would listen with an open mind. She couldn't bear it if the man she loved— because damn it, she was beginning to believe that was the truth—wouldn't forgive her son.

The door opened before she could knock. The alley was shadowed and dim and she squinted at the bright Sunday sunlight streaming through the wide window behind Cash.

It had become her custom to breeze in with a smile and a kiss. Today, she hesitated on the landing, uncertain of her welcome. "Hi. I brought your stuff back." She held out the bag.

Without speaking, he took it, and then stepped back. She accepted the implied invitation, walking past, twisting her now empty hands together.

He stared at her with a blank expression, still holding the bag. His eyes were flat, uncompromising, with dark purple pockets underneath that made him look ill. His beard, usually neatly brushed, sprouted unruly hairs, and the thick strands on his skull were messy and unkempt.

"Are you okay?" She reached toward him, concern flaring.

He retreated with abrupt steps, bumping to a stop against the kitchen counter. "Fine." His gravel voice was more hoarse than usual, as if he hadn't spoken for days.

She lowered her hand. Something more than fury must have caused such a rapid and drastic physical change. "Are you sure? You look terrible."

A flare blazed in the depths of his grey eyes. Not anger. Pain? Longing? She wasn't sure. "I said I'm fine." As if suddenly aware of the bag in his hands, he placed it on the floor.

"It wasn't meant as an insult, Cash. I-I care about you." A horrific thought struck her. "It's not Elle, is it? She's not...injured? Cyril was texting with her this morning. He didn't say anything." If Elle had been assaulted, would she have admitted it to Cyril?

He shrugged, which hopefully meant Elle was okay, at least physically. Drawing himself up, he squared his shoulders as if preparing for battle. "You wanted to talk?"

"Yes." She also wanted to comfort him, but his posture warned her to keep away. She regrouped and focused on why she'd come. "I talked with Cyril. He told me why they were at the party. Why he was drunk."

Cash grunted.

She licked her dry lips and continued. "TJ threatened him. Said if he didn't bring Elle to the party that night, he'd get his gang together and trash your shop. Worse this time."

Cash's fingers twitched, but he didn't say anything. She plowed on.

"Cyril knows your burglar alarm isn't linked with any security services, which he learned when you asked him to lock up once. He should have called and told us what TJ intended, but thought he could handle it without anyone finding out." He'd also admitted this wasn't the first time he and TJ had met since they'd broken into Cash's shop. She was still reeling at that deception. It was going to take a long time before she could trust him again. "When they got there, TJ started pestering Elle. Cyril warned him off, but he kept at her. They both wanted to leave, but Cyril was afraid of what TJ and his friends would do if they did. Then TJ made him a deal. He'd leave Elle alone if Cyril could beat him in a drinking competition. About five shots in, when he realized he wasn't going to win, he told Elle to lock herself in the bathroom and call you."

Cash smoothed his beard in his familiar gesture. "Idiot."

"Yes. But he thought he was doing the right thing."

"The right thing would have been to let me handle it."

"Like you handled that man you punched?" She pressed a hand to her mouth to stop any further words escaping. She hadn't been able to get the vision of Cash's fist slamming into the fat man's face out of her head. She'd felt the same rage, the same need to punish, but she'd controlled her response. Cash hadn't.

He sucked in a breath like her fist had landed in his stomach. "That man was Tyrone, TJ's father. And he's the real reason Cyril and Elle were at the party."

She frowned. "What do you mean?"

"He wanted revenge on me. Cyril and Elle were just a means to an end. It was me he really wanted to hurt."

There. He'd done it. Ripped the bandage off.

Penta regarded him with a puzzled expression, teeth worrying her bottom lip. "I don't understand."

Cash had expected her to start today's conversation with *it's not you, it's me.* When she hadn't, when her first words had been concern about his appearance, his heart had kicked with a jolt of joy. He'd had to remind himself that breaking up was best for her and hadn't allowed himself to weaken. When she'd revealed how Cyril had been compelled to bring Elle to the party, how he'd risked his own life to protect her—all because of Cash—it had only strengthened his resolve.

"Middle of July, I went back to the bar. The one where I almost killed a man." Might as well be blunt. It would make it easier for Penta to accept reality. "Don't know why I did. Hadn't been back since I got out. Tyrone was there. We used to be friends. Grew up together. A while later, he comes to the shop, offers to bring me biker gang business. I refused, told him I didn't need or want it. Must have pissed him off more than I realized. Elle and Cyril came in while he was there. Tyrone recognized Cyril as one of TJ's buddies. That probably gave him the idea. How to punish me." Thank god Penta hadn't been there. Tyrone might have felt some restraint even as he used kids to get his revenge. If he'd known about Penta, knew that Cash loved her, who knew what nightmare he might have come up with.

As he waited stoically for Penta to come to the obvious conclusion, he had time to consider that revelation.

He loved Penta. The thought of losing her made

him feel hollow, empty, numb. But dragging her deeper into the fiasco that was his life was not an option. He had to let her go.

"Let me get this straight." Penta reached behind her, found the back of the sofa, and leaned against it. "TJ threatened to wreck your shop to force Cyril and Elle to come to the party. And he did that because his father wanted to punish you for refusing to work for criminals?"

He worked his way through that and nodded.

"What a fucking asshole!" She exploded off the couch, fists flying, curls bouncing. "He took your friendship and turned it against you, then put our kids in danger. I'm going to kill him!"

Cash gaped. He'd never heard Penta curse before. And realizing her fury wasn't directed at himself made him dizzy.

He loved her so much. Too bad it didn't matter.

"We have to stop seeing each other, Penta." He tasted iron in his mouth, as if the words made his gums bleed. "It's over. It's all over."

Chapter Twenty-Nine

Penta's furious gesticulations froze. "What? Why?"

He didn't want to spell it out, but knew it was the only way to get her to agree. She wasn't the type to give up, not Penta. Not even when giving up was what she should do.

"Linda was right, all these years. Right to keep me from Elle. I've barely been in her life two months and she was almost raped."

Penta flinched. He loved that she wore rose-coloured glasses, but it was time she took them off.

He spoke harshly, determined to make her see. "It doesn't matter how hard I try to escape it. My past will always be there, ready to ruin the lives of people I love."

"But that's not—"

"Don't." He held his palm toward her like a traffic cop. "Don't say it's not fair or that it doesn't matter. It's the truth. Why do you think Cyril brought Elle to the party?"

Her brow furrowed. "I told you. To save your shop from being vandalized again."

"No. He did it because he's scared of me. If he felt safe, trusted me, he would have told us. Instead, he thought he had to handle it on his own because he was frightened of what I might do. Maybe not to him, but to his friends."

"They're not his friends." Her tone was flat,

determined, as if saying it would make it so. And maybe on the surface she was right. But underneath, where it counted, she was wrong.

Cyril was bound to those degenerates for the rest of his life, just like Cash was bound to Tyrone. The only chance he had to break free would be if Cash was out of his life. Which meant out of Penta's.

Her lips puffed belligerently. "You're wrong about Cyril being scared of you. He respects you, maybe even more than he does me. You've been a good influence on him, not a bad one."

He closed his eyes briefly, lanced to the core by her misplaced compliments. She was making it so much harder. If she wouldn't admit that breaking off their relationship was the best for everyone, he would have to accomplish his goal using another tactic. One he'd hoped desperately to avoid.

He would have to send her away. And he knew just the buttons to press.

Speaking as bitterly, as coldly, as he knew how, he said, "Are you going to discipline him for going to the party?"

She stiffened, rearing back, her chin lifting. "I think his hangover was punishment enough. Besides, he had the best of intentions. Everything he did, he did to protect others. Why would I punish him for that?"

"The best way to protect Elle would have been to leave her alone. And I can take care of myself and my shop." He felt sick using this weapon, but he had to make Penta abandon him, needed her so furious she would never want to see him again.

"Well, of course, but—"

He launched the killing blow. "Maybe if you'd paid more attention to him, none of this would have happened."

She paled and staggered, as if he had landed a physical punch. "How can you say that?"

"Easily." He almost gagged at the lie. "You were with me having a dirty weekend when you should have been at home keeping an eye on your delinquent son."

Her voice trembled, bewilderment pinching the corners of her eyes. "B-but you said I had to let him grow up. Let him make his own mistakes."

"Yeah, but that was before his mistakes almost got my daughter assaulted." Forcing his feet to move, he opened the door. "You should leave now."

Penta went.

Her mind a blank, she drove home, opened the garage, parked neatly beside the empty space where Felix's car went, got out of the van, closed the overhead door, went inside the house—

—and came to a halt in the kitchen, unsure of what to do next.

The safe familiar space seemed alien, foreign. Or maybe that was the wasteland inside her.

Cash's ferocity had smashed everything she knew about herself, everything she'd tried to be, into tiny, agonized fragments.

He'd accused her of ignoring her child. Of putting herself before her son's well-being.

It was an unfathomable concept.

She needed time to think. Time to process what had just happened. She'd gone to Cash knowing there might be an argument, a disagreement. She hadn't fooled herself into thinking he'd be pleased by Cyril's explanations and excuses. But she'd never dreamed he'd kick her out, break off their relationship, accuse her of being neglectful.

Her brain kept short-circuiting, her fingers trembling with overwhelming emotion.

She had no idea how long she stood there before Cyril came bounding up from the basement. He showed no signs of yesterday's incapacitation, displaying the exasperating resilience of youth. Barely tossing her a glance, he headed for the fridge.

"What's for dinner?" He loaded his arms with

packages of deli meat, cheese, mustard, and mayo, nudged the door shut with his elbow, and placed everything on the counter.

She shook herself out of her fugue, watching with bemusement as he set about making his mid-afternoon snack. "I don't know."

Cyril paused in the motion of extracting four slices of bread from the plastic-wrapped loaf. "Are you okay?"

"Of course." It took supreme effort to smile reassuringly.

Apparently, the attempt was wasted. If anything, Cyril's concern deepened. "Are you sure? You look kinda pale."

She *felt* pale. As if all the colour had leached from her life, washed away by Cash's accusations and rejection. "Maybe I'm coming down with something. I might have a nap."

"You *never* nap." Cyril abandoned his sandwich-making and approached. "Weren't you going to see Cash today?"

The knot lodged under her breastbone ascended into her throat. She spoke around it, half-choking. "I did. He understands. He doesn't blame you anymore." No. His blame had shifted to her, a thought that continued to confuse and befuddle her.

Cyril squinted, focused and intent. "That's good, right? Why do you look so sad, then?"

"It has nothing to do with Cash." *It has everything to do with Cash.* She couldn't help it. Tears welled and the back of her nose burned. She sniffed and turned to the sink, dampening a cloth and wiping the already clean counter. "I'm just missing the girls, I guess."

"Mom." Cyril's tone was so gentle, so...*adult* that she almost sobbed. "Did you and Cash break up? Is it my fault?"

She spun on her heel. "No," she said fiercely. "Well, yes, we broke up. But it is *not* your fault."

"Then why? I thought you liked him."

"I do." *I love him.* Much good that did her now. "He thought it was for the best."

"*He* did? He dumped *you*?"

Her son's incredulity should have been flattering and funny, but she didn't smile. Couldn't. "I guess he did."

"That asshole!"

She couldn't summon the energy to reprimand him for language she had so recently used herself. "It's his prerogative, Cyril. He's allowed to decide who he does and doesn't date. It doesn't make him an...what you said."

"Well, he is. And I'm sorry he upset you." Cyril raised his arms, hesitated, and then hugged her.

She couldn't remember the last time he'd initiated an embrace. He was thin and reedy, but his shoulders were square and his arms wiry. Her cheek pressed against his collarbone, and she felt a familiar shock as she rediscovered her son was taller than her.

"I'll be okay." She whispered the words, a promise made to herself as much as to Cyril. "I'll be okay."

Chapter Thirty

After Penta left, Cash got drunk.

It was a deliberate decision. He didn't have anything other than a couple beers in the apartment, so made a special trip to buy a bottle of whiskey. By the time he was holed up again, a summer storm had rolled in. The heat wave broke with a thunderous crash, a fusillade of rain attacking his front window.

He didn't bother with a glass. The first swallow burned, leaving him gasping from its long-forgotten bite. The second went down easier. He didn't bother counting after the third.

Monday morning, he woke with a head that boomed as if the remnants of last night's tempest had found refuge there. He lay stomach down on his sofa, one arm hanging off the side, the other crushed beneath his chest. Through one half-open eye, he spied the bottle of hell water on the floor within arm's reach. It was half full.

God. When had he become such a lightweight? That amount of booze shouldn't have destroyed him this badly.

Then he remembered Penta and how he'd sent her away and wondered if his current state had more to do with losing her than the whiskey.

Dragging himself upright, he found the cap for the bottle, sealed it, and placed it in the cupboard above the fridge. Then he took a long hot shower and, feeling almost human as a result, soaked up any alcohol still swirling in his gut with four pieces of toast.

After that, he had nothing to do but contemplate the desert of his life.

He'd been perfectly fine on his own—before Elle, before Penta. If he could forget the last two months, he'd be fine again.

He should really get back to work on the Baby Bonnie. It was so close to being done. Yet, he couldn't bear to touch it. The plans he'd made to roar down the highway with Penta riding the Bonnie at his side taunted him. He should have known better than to hope for such joy in his future.

Also, his shop was riddled with the ghosts of both Penta and Elle, and the thought of spending a day with them as his only company made him growl in frustration.

He'd have to get over that. Tomorrow.

Today, he'd clear his head with a visit to Camp Chance.

He took his truck instead of his bike. Memories of Penta followed him there, though it had been weeks since he'd brought her and he'd returned alone several times between then and now. He never neglected his commitment to the youth patching their lives back together, no matter how busy he was, so he'd already spent hours in the very workshop where she had kissed him.

The kiss that had changed everything. As he parked outside the main building, he admitted the truth of that.

Penta had changed everything. She'd accepted him—his struggles and sins, his failings and faults. He hadn't asked her to, but she had anyway.

A group of teenage boys emerged from one of the residences and sauntered to the peeled log pavilion. He watched them dully for a moment, stroking his beard, gathering the energy to get out, to walk to the workshop.

He'd done his best to redeem his past mistakes.

Staying away from Elle, volunteering at Camp Chance, keeping his head down and his nose clean—it had all been his way of making reparations for a life lived on the edge of lawlessness. And for two brief months, he thought he'd done enough. Thought maybe, just maybe, he'd paid the full price.

One of the camp counselors stepped out of the main building and waved an enthusiastic greeting in his direction.

At least he was still welcome here. He climbed out and waved back.

He might have given up on himself, but he wasn't giving up on these kids. If he could keep one—just *one*—from making the same mistakes he had, it would all be worth it.

Felix and Cyril were both out of the house. That didn't stop Penta from taking her laptop and hiding in her bedroom. She had decisions to make and needed privacy to make them.

She clicked through to the program page on the College of New Caledonia website. It was a wonder her computer didn't do it automatically, as she'd visited it frequently since her confrontation with Cash.

The first two days, she'd spent far too much time with her comforter stuffed in her mouth muffling her sobs, desperate to hide the depths of her despair from her sons. Her bones ached with the effort it took to appear normal. Between Cash's rejection and the pain of missing her daughters, she'd felt a ghost of her usual self.

One positive had come out of her agony. She'd finally learned her lesson. Loving someone didn't give her the right or the ability to control them. She loved Cash with an intensity that frightened her, and he hadn't returned that love. He'd made his own choice, just as her children would have to make theirs.

And she had to make hers.

She'd discovered the Medical Laboratory Technician diploma program by accident. Unlike so many of the jobs and courses she'd reviewed over the summer, she knew in her bones she'd be good at it, that she'd enjoy it.

Seats were limited and she had no idea how her qualifications would compare to someone fresh out of high school. But she'd never know unless she tried.

It was time to reclaim Penta Unleashed, even if she felt a pale imitation without Cash by her side.

With a deep breath, she started typing.

A few hours later, Penta joined the rest of the Silverberries at Helen and Nathan's lakeside cabin. Their August event was an all-day affair marking the anniversary of the first time they had discarded serious book talk for more adventurous pursuits.

The rain and cooler temperatures of last Sunday's storm hadn't lasted forty-eight hours, and Penta was sweating, despite wearing nothing but a one-piece navy-blue bathing suit and lying in the protective shade of a large patio umbrella. She and Terrance had claimed the loungers on a deck overhanging the beach, while other members of the club, including their hosts, played in the water and lazed on the dock below.

"You're rather quiet, my dear." In concession to the searing temperatures, Terrance had removed his silk scarf. He used it now to blot his upper lip. His khaki shorts were stiff with starch, his collared shirt a jaunty blue, and his bare feet protected by uncreased deck shoes.

"Am I?" She sipped her iced orange juice and placed it on the small table between them. While her last painful scene with Cash played almost constantly in her mind, forming a barrier between her and the real world, it now vied for precedence over the application she'd submitted earlier that day. Her mind ping-ponged between the two with a ferocity that presaged a headache later. "It's this heat."

"Liar. I know you better than that. Tell Uncle Terrance all."

It was his usual invitation, the lightly humorous tone and wording giving her the space to accept or reject without censure.

She wasn't ready to talk about going back to school. She might not get accepted and, if so, wanted no one to know about her attempt. As for Cash, she was afraid she might burst into tears if she mentioned his name. Her only option was to change the topic, so answered with a question of her own. "How's Bennett?"

Terrance flicked a non-existent speck from his shorts. "I wouldn't know. He moved out."

"What?" Penta bolted upright and swung her bare feet to the wooden deck. "When? Why didn't you tell me?"

"A couple of weeks ago. And I was hoping he'd come back so I wouldn't have to tell anyone at all." He kept his face averted, but now that she looked at him, really looked, she could see the signs of strain around his mouth and eyes, the pasty texture of his skin.

"I'm so sorry." Maybe Cash's brutal accusations had been right. Had her infatuation with him caused her to become oblivious to everyone else?

"Yes. Me, too."

She patted his hand in a pathetic gesture of sympathy. "I thought things were getting better. What happened?"

Terrance shrugged and smoothed the thinning hair on his scalp. "You know he is more than fifteen years younger than me?"

She nodded, not quite seeing the point but willing to let him explain in his own way.

"We've been together since he was twenty-two. Married when he was twenty-four. It would have been our tenth anniversary this December."

She squeezed his forearm, offering wordless comfort.

"He says that he was too young when we married to know what he really wanted in life. That he needs the chance to meet other people, do other things. That our life is too regimented, too structured." Terrance's voice was colourless. It was such a dramatic change from his usual flamboyant gaiety Penta shivered.

She shifted onto the edge of his lounger and wrapped her arms around his shoulders. He tucked his face into her neck and embraced her tightly. He made no sound, but his shoulders shook with tiny tremors, and she knew the dampness on her collarbone wasn't only sweat.

After a few minutes, he drew back and wiped his eyes with his scarf. "Don't tell anyone else, will you? I'm not ready for them to know."

"Of course not." She scooted back to her own seat. "Maybe it will still work out. He might just need some time away."

"Maybe." His eyes held little hope, but he offered a tentative smile. "Don't think I didn't notice."

"Notice what?"

"You didn't answer my question. Your turn to bare your soul."

Her own misfortune didn't compare to the dissolution of a marriage. After all, she'd gone through that. She knew the difference between a divorce and a breakup. The hollow emptiness she was feeling now only seemed worse than what she'd experienced when Mark left because it was fresher, unmuted by time.

At least, that's what she kept telling herself.

Terrance was watching her, despair and loneliness darkening his expression. Maybe her story would distract him from his own misery for a minute or two.

"Cash and I broke up." It was her turn to avoid eye contact. She picked up her orange juice, drained the last drops, and then fidgeted with the empty glass.

"That marvellously grim ginger? I thought things

were getting serious between you."

So had she. "Yes, well, that was before Cyril and Elle ran into serious trouble." By the time she'd recounted the events of that terrible night and the Sunday after, Terrance's eyes were round, his mouth open in a startled O.

"He accused you of ignoring Cyril? What an idiotic thing to say." His clear rejection of this assertion soothed a small part of Penta's soul. "I suppose you see the irony here? Not that it's much consolation, of course."

"Irony?"

"Mark accused you of neglecting him for the children. Now Cash accuses you of ignoring your children to be with him."

That aspect of the situation hadn't occurred to her. "You're right. It's not much consolation. If I'm honest, Mark probably had a genuine grievance. I did take him for granted. But he should have talked to me about it, explained what he was feeling, so we could work on our marriage together. He decided it was easier to quit."

"And what about Cash?" Terrance queried. "Was he right, to any degree?"

Chapter Thirty-One

Penta had thought of little else all week. "It's not fair," she burst out. "When we first met, he accused me of being hyper-vigilant, of coddling Cyril, of protecting them all too much. Then he says I *ignore* them? He can't have it both ways, can he?"

"Why would he say it if he doesn't believe it? If he wanted to break up with you, why not just say so, instead of making up illogical excuses?" Terrance's gaze was soft yet direct.

"He did say so. Said he was a poor influence, and we shouldn't see each other anymore. But that's rubbish."

"If that's how he feels…"

She waved her hand as if swatting a mosquito. "He's a good man. I don't know why he doesn't see that."

"It's often harder to see our good points than our bad. But that doesn't mean our feelings of inadequacy should be dismissed." She had the uncomfortable feeling he was disappointed with her and was thankful when he moved on. "What about this Tyrone? You say he's a friend of Cash?"

"Not anymore. Cash is certain Cyril and Elle were put in danger as a way to get back at him. But nothing would have happened if Cyril had let us know what was going on, so it's more his fault than Cash's."

"Would your fellow see it that way, though? If he'd said yes to Tyrone's proposal, there would have been no reason to pressure Cyril. In his mind, the evil starts there."

Talking this out had reminded her of something else, something she'd forgotten in the pain and sorrow of rejection. "He mentioned his past, more than once. Said it would always be there, ready to ruin the lives of people he loved." She stared at Terrance. "I thought he was only talking about Elle. But maybe—" She broke off, afraid to finish her thought.

Terrance had no such compunction. "Maybe he was talking about you? About loving you?"

She opened her mouth and closed it again, wordless with shock.

And hope.

"Don't throw love away, Penta." Terrance's voice quavered, and he pressed his lips together before continuing. "We both know how precious it is. You need to talk to this man of yours. Sort things out. Don't let a misunderstanding ruin what you could have together."

Cash forced himself to operate the shop at the usual hours all week. Forced himself to speak politely to customers. Forced himself to continue the restoration of the Baby Bonnie, though it brought him no joy. But just because Penta would never have a chance to appreciate its beauty, that didn't mean someone else shouldn't. Also, it was a painful reminder of the last months, and he wanted it out of his shop, out of his life.

On Saturday, he locked the front door, wishing the action could also lock out the dragging depression dogging him. He hadn't made it to the rear hall before a knock on the glass halted his steps. His first instinct was to keep going, ignore whoever the latecomer was. But they would have seen him, and he didn't have a good excuse for avoiding them.

Shoulders slumping, he turned back to the front.

Linda and Elle stood outside. His heart swelled, choking him, and a ripple of goosebumps shivered across his chest.

They were probably here to berate him for his role in last weekend's near disaster. To declare to his face that he was dead to them. But he didn't care. He'd thought he would never see Elle again. Being near her one more time was worth whatever happened next.

Linda rapped again and made a *come here* motion. Elle stood tucked in behind her, staring at the ground, long loose hair hiding her face.

He approached, unlocked the door, and moved back so they could enter.

"I hope it's okay we just showed up. I texted you earlier, but you didn't reply." Linda jutted her chin sideways in the gesture she'd bequeathed to Elle. Her tone was gentle. He didn't trust it.

"I was working." Also, he avoided the phone whenever possible. Otherwise, he did nothing but stare at the screen as if the force of his will could make a text from Penta appear. He'd never expected to hear from Linda or Elle. But even though he was the one who had chased her away, his stupid heart wouldn't let him accept Penta was truly gone.

"Well." Linda rested a hand on Elle's shoulder and glanced from their daughter to Cash and back again. "Elle has something she'd like to say."

She had yet to look at him. God, she must hate him so much. Why had Linda brought her here? Maybe it was something about closure or standing up for herself. It didn't matter. He wouldn't make it harder for her. He wouldn't defend himself, wouldn't try to justify his actions. He braced himself to accept his sentence.

When Elle raised her head, her eyes were glazed with tears. The choking sensation returned, along with an impotent fury. *He* was the reason for her distress, and he hated himself for that.

"I'm sorry." Her voice trembled. "I know I

shouldn't have gone to the party. I should have made Cyril tell Mom or you what was going on. If I had, he wouldn't have gotten so sick. You can die from alcohol poisoning, you know. What if he'd died?" The words tumbled as fast and furious as whitewater in a canyon and her voice rose to a near shriek. "It's all my fault, and I know you hate me for being so stupid. But I'm sorry. I'm so, so sorry. I don't want to lose you. I just found you."

He stood motionless under the barrage, unable to process what she was saying. Her confession was so unexpected, so completely beyond the realm of anything he'd contemplated that for several moments he wasn't sure she was speaking English.

She's going to break your heart in ways you can't even imagine. He hadn't fully understood the wisdom in the words Penta had written in his Father's Day card until now. Elle's pain was his pain, her fear his fear, her sorrow his sorrow.

He was so stunned he couldn't speak. Could do nothing but open his arms.

Elle leaped into his embrace. She pressed her cheek to his chest and continued to speak, sentences running together so quickly they were nothing but random syllables, incomprehensibly muffled against his shirt.

"Shhhh." He rubbed his hand up and down her back, her shoulders heaving with her shuddering, gasping breaths and torrent of speech. "Shhhh. I'm not going anywhere. I thought you'd never want to see me again."

Her arms tightened on his waist. "Of course I want to see you. You won't send me away, will you?"

"What do you mean, send you away?" He groped for the meaning in her words, still dazed by her revelations.

"I know you're mad at me, but I thought you'd give me a chance to explain, to say I'm sorry. But you haven't called or texted all week. I thought..." Sobs mangled the next words beyond recognition.

She thought he'd abandoned her. Shunned her. When all he'd wanted, ever, was to know her as a father should know a daughter.

"You have nothing to be sorry for." He gripped her shoulders and pushed her away a fraction. "Look at me, Elle. Please, sweetie, just look at me."

She raised her head. Seeing the desperate distress in her miserable expression was one thousand times worse than hearing it. He was gutted, hollowed out, shaking. He dipped his knees so they were eye to eye. "I'm the one that should be apologizing. None of this was your fault. Cyril told you why he wanted you to go to the party, didn't he?"

He addressed the words to Elle but watched Linda as he spoke. He couldn't believe she'd brought Elle to him. He'd thought she would jump at the chance to alienate him from their daughter. Instead, she was the catalyst to their reconciliation.

Her eyes were also sheened with tears, and she sniffed before replying. "He's an idiot, but can you blame him? He didn't want to put you in jeopardy."

"No, just our daughter." His sarcastic tone shocked him. *I guess I'm still angry with him. Huh.* He pulled Elle tighter, needing to feel her close.

"She put herself in jeopardy." Linda shot her a wry glance. She had huddled against Cash's chest again and didn't see it. "We've had several discussions about that, haven't we?"

Elle nodded, her silky hair catching on Cash's beard.

"I gave Tyrone a reason." He didn't want to, but he had to say it, put it all out there. "You were right to keep me away all these years. It kept her safe. Look what happened the minute you let me in."

Linda shook her head. "This didn't happen because you are in Elle's life now. This happened because you turned down a chance to make money off a gang and a vicious pathetic man decided to use children in a vindictive game."

"I should have realized something like this would happen if I went back to my old neighbourhood."

"You're omniscient now?" The familiar biting edge was back in her voice. It soothed him. Things were returning to normal if Linda was pissed.

"Tyrone had forgotten all about me until he saw me there."

"And he could have looked you up online and walked into your shop any day." Linda quirked one corner of her mouth up. "Do you think he'll try something else?"

"I don't know. I hope it was more of a prank than a true wish to injure anyone."

"Well, Elle and Cyril will be smarter next time. And let's hope that he's lost his taste for payback." She grinned, baring her teeth in savage satisfaction. "Elle says you made his nose bleed."

"I'm sorry she saw that." He kissed the top of her head in apology.

"I'm not." Elle's tone echoed her mother's grim glee. "Once Cyril told me everything, I wished you'd punched him harder."

Shocked into laughter by her bloodthirstiness, he wrapped her tighter in his arms.

And for the first time in more than a week, he drew a full, deep, cleansing breath.

Chapter Thirty-Two

Staggered by the complete reversal Elle and Linda's visit had wrought, Cash diffidently suggested they stay for dinner. When they agreed, his appetite returned with a roar, and no scrap remained of either of the two large pizzas he ordered by the time the two women left later that evening.

Conversation had been tentative at first. The detente between him and Linda was fragile, but for the first time he sensed she was willing to try and get along. She even accepted his goodbye kiss on the cheek with a slight twinkle and no cynical comment.

With a full belly and the memory of Elle's shining eyes to lull him to sleep, he zoned out for twelve hours. When he woke up late Sunday morning, his first thought was of Penta.

Was there the possibility, no matter how slight, that he might be able to fix things with her too? If Elle and Linda could forgive him, could she?

Or had he already been granted more absolution than he deserved?

He decided to start off small, with a text to Cyril. He fussed with the wording for far too long before finally growling and sending the simplest message he could.

I'm sorry about what happened with Tyrone. Call me?

The dancing dots flickered. It was okay if the boy didn't want to talk. He'd take a text. At least it would be a start.

The dots flickered and vanished, flickered and vanished. He was startled when the phone rang. Cyril's name appeared on the screen.

He answered, palms sweaty, chest aching, breath short. Thank god he'd started with the boy. If he'd contacted Penta, he might have had a real heart attack. "Hey."

"You made my mom cry." The youthful voice held a mature sharpness.

Fuck. "I'm sorry."

"You're sorry for a lot of things, aren't you?"

"You have no idea."

"I never thought you'd hurt her. I thought you liked her."

Cash suddenly recalled his promise to Felix the night Penta had gone home with him for the first time. *I promise not to hurt your mother.* At the time, he'd thought Felix was worried in the physical sense. It had never dawned on him he might have the power to hurt her emotionally.

"I do. I like her a lot." Cash rubbed the bridge of his nose where a headache was brewing. Here went nothing. "Actually...I think I love her."

Silence.

More silence.

Then—

"Does she know?"

"Not yet. I want to tell her. To ask for a second chance. But I don't know if she'll return my calls."

"You hurt her bad. I was pretty young when she and Dad split, but I remember what she was like. This was worse."

What kind of an asshole found hope in that statement? "I want to make it up to her. *Need* to make it up. Any suggestions?"

The quiet purr of a slowly driven vehicle droned through Penta's closed bedroom window. The engine cut out and she wondered, not really caring, which neighbour was getting a late-night visitor.

She flopped into a new position and closed her eyes, determined to sleep. In the seven and a half nights since Cash had pushed her away, she'd discovered a new sympathy for insomniacs. And after her talk with Terrance the day before, she had even more to keep her awake.

Was it possible Cash loved her? At least enough to be worried for her safety and to protect her the only way he knew how—by keeping his distance?

She couldn't live with the uncertainty. She had to know what he felt and, if revealing her own emotions was the only way, she'd risk the humiliation.

Tomorrow morning—a glance at the clock revealed it was after midnight—no, *this* morning, she would be waiting at the door of his shop when it opened. He couldn't refuse to talk to her if she was standing in front of him, could he?

As she punched her pillow into a more comfortable shape, she heard the muted click of the front door opening and closing. Sitting upright, she listened intently. Had she imagined it?

No. Voices drifted up the stairs and through her open bedroom door. Was it Felix, coming home from another date with Hadiyyah? She had yet to meet the girl. Was he sneaking her into the house?

Padding barefooted across the carpet, she peered down the hall. No more voices, but shuffling and rustling sounds. Then a grunt of effort and a soft thud.

If a grunt could sound like someone, this one sounded like Cash. She put it down to wishful thinking. She'd "seen" him multiple times during the last lonely week, only to be disillusioned.

Cautiously, she stepped out of her room and shuffled to the top of the stairs.

Was that fresh-baked cookies she smelled? She sniffed deeply. Yes. Chocolate chip. *What on earth...?*

"Put it there."

Her heart leaped into her throat, skin prickling. *Cash.* She hadn't been imagining things. There was no mistaking that gravelly tone.

A solid thunk, and then more shuffling and rustling.

She tiptoed down the stairs, through the short hall leading from the front door—closed and locked, she noted—to the kitchen.

And froze at the sight that greeted her.

Cash didn't know how Penta made her cookies look so smoothly rounded. His were oddly shaped and lumpy, even though he'd followed the recipe in the handmade book she'd given him with precision. He'd sampled one—just to make sure it wouldn't poison her—and it had tasted pretty close to hers. Whatever. They would have to do. He'd arranged them on the tray as neatly as he could, but they'd shifted during the drive. He pushed one back into place with a fingertip.

Cyril adjusted the huge bouquet of flowers Cash had also brought, spinning it so the card was clearly visible. "How's this?" he whispered.

Cash nodded. The cookies and flowers had been Cyril's idea. But he had another ace up his sleeve, one he hoped would be a powerful symbol of his repentance.

"What's going on?"

He spun around and drank in his first sight of Penta in more than a week.

Her pajamas were thin and silky but not the teapot ones he loved to tease her about. These were a pale grey that brought out the silvery strands in her tousled dark brown curls. He could tell with a glance she was braless beneath the buttoned top. His pulse, already thready with nerves, accelerated.

Cyril slid toward the door leading downstairs. "Just listen to him, Mom, okay?" He vanished.

Cash's skin felt like it had shrunk two sizes. He

rolled his shoulders to alleviate the sensation. "How are you?"

Her gaze skittered from the cookies to the flowers and back to him. "Confused." She took a couple steps closer.

But not close enough. He desperately wanted to take her in his arms, to feel her pressed against him, preferably skin to skin, but he had some grovelling to do first. "You look tired."

She raised an eyebrow.

He winced. "Sorry. I'm messing this up."

She took another step. "It's okay. I am tired." One more step. "I haven't been sleeping well."

"Me, neither." His feet remained glued in place as he willed her to keep coming. Every inch nearer raised his hope another degree. "I'm sorry we woke you. You weren't supposed to hear. I wanted you to find this in the morning. I wrote a card." He pointed at the white envelope tucked into the bouquet.

She tilted her head, a corner of her mouth lifting. "Well, since I'm here now...?"

He tried to remember what he'd written. He'd spent hours finding the right words.

Nothing. His mind was blank. Penta's small smile faded.

"I said horrible things," he blurted. "I wanted to apologize."

Her shoulders drooped, just a fraction, as if she'd expected something else and was disappointed. "That's what the flowers and cookies are? An apology?"

"Yes. And there's more." He held out his hand. "Come with me?"

"Where? I'm in my pajamas."

"Just to the front door."

She stared at his hand. When she took it, tentative but willing, tears burned the back of his throat. He swallowed hard. God, he'd missed her touch.

Leading her to the entrance, he unlocked the door,

opened it, and tugged her onto the step. The night breeze held a slight chill, and she shivered. He wanted to cuddle her, share his warmth, but refrained.

He pointed to the box of his pickup. "I want you to have the Baby Bonnie."

Chapter Thirty-Three

Secure in her restraints, the Tiger Cub had ridden to Penta's like a queen in her carriage—elegant, regal, and mysterious. Her chrome and bright red paint gleamed in the moonlight, a beautiful sight. But nowhere near as beautiful as the rumpled, sleepy, bemused woman standing next to him.

"I had planned to unload her, leave her for you to find in the morning. I couldn't drive her over because I needed the truck to bring the cookies and flowers. Hard to carry that on a bike. And I didn't want to walk home, either."

Cash knew he was rambling. Penta's unnatural silence and statue-like stillness unnerved him. Her eyes never left the Bonnie, and her lips were slightly parted, as if stunned.

Finally, she drew her gaze away and looked at him. "You want me to have her? I've watched you work on her all summer. You love that bike. I was sure you were going to keep her for yourself."

"Even if you turn around and sell her tomorrow, I want to know she was yours, at least for a little while. I want you to have her. Because she reminds me of you."

"What do you mean?"

"She's strong and beautiful, and so are you. She's meant to go places and have adventures, and so should you. Penta Unleashed, remember? I'm so sorry I accused you of ignoring your kids. That was cruel.

And wrong. So wrong. You're a good mom, and I shouldn't have used your love as a weapon."

Her lips trembled, but just for an instant. "Why did you, then?"

"I was trying to protect you. I didn't want Tyrone to use you like he used the kids. Didn't want my past to ruin anything more than it already had. I had to send you away, no matter what it took."

A breeze fluttered her curls, and she shivered.

"Let's go inside." He drew her back, shut the door, and paused, unsure of where to go next.

Penta guided him to the living room, pushed him into the upholstered chair, and climbed into his lap.

The fragile hope flickering in his chest flamed higher. With a rumbling sigh, he wrapped his arms around her and rested his chin on her crown.

"I understand." Her words were soft, a bare breath. "For a long time now, you've been told that to keep those you love safe you have to stay away. But I don't want you to stay away, Cash. I'd rather be with you, no matter what the trials and troubles, than be without you."

The stone in his throat threatened to choke him. He swallowed, trying to dislodge it, but couldn't. The words he wanted to say, words he was terrified to say, jammed up behind it, unspoken.

"Thank you for the Baby Bonnie. I appreciate the gesture, I really do." Her fingers stroked his beard as she kept her head tucked under his chin. "But I can't accept her. She belongs with you."

"You said I love that bike, and you're right. I do." Suddenly, the blockage in his throat dissolved and the words slipped out—easy, right, and peaceful. "But I love you more."

The joyous sobs Penta had been stifling for several minutes escaped. Her emotions ran so high she thought her chest would burst. Far too aware of Cyril on the floor below, she kept her lips pressed together and buried her face in Cash's neck. The zippers on his leather riding jacket dug into her in uncomfortable places, but she didn't care.

His arms banded around her shaking shoulders. "Don't cry. Oh, god, please don't cry. I take it back if it upsets you so much. I take it back."

She reared up and punched his shoulder. "Don't you dare. You can't take it back now. You said it. You love me."

He regarded her with such a conflicted expression a hysterical giggle bubbled through the easing sobs. His brows lowered, masculine confusion written all over his face, and apparently decided silence was his best option.

"I love you too." Penta brushed her fingertips across the lips half-hidden behind his beard. "I love you so much. So, you can't take it back. You said it, and I'm holding you to it."

With a suddenness that had her gasping, he rose to his feet, staggered the two steps toward the sofa, and dropped her onto it. His heavy solidness followed, covering her like a weighted blanket, and then his mouth was on hers.

His promises of passion mingled with profanities ravished her soul as his caresses worshipped her body. She drifted, delirious after a week of doubt and depression, whispering her own words of assurance. It was only when his hand slipped inside the waistband of her pajama bottoms and dipped into her wetness that a shred of sanity returned.

"Cyril. Downstairs." She arched, encouraging his fingers deeper. At some point, his jacket had been tossed to the floor and his jeans unzipped. She worked her own hand under his boxer briefs and gripped his hard hot shaft. "Might hear us. Bedroom?"

He hissed and thrust his hips. "Ask me to stay, Penta. Ask me."

"Stay, Cash. Always."

Cash couldn't wait to show Penta what her commitment meant to him.

They stumbled up the stairs to her room, his hands on her waist urging her forward. Inside, he nudged the door closed with his heel. She spun in his grasp, her silky pajamas cool and slippery, and raised up on tiptoe.

He lowered his head and took her offered mouth. Their lips clung and slid in a delirious dance. Her taste infused his blood with comfort and lust.

"God, I missed you." He muttered the words against the plush softness of her cheek as he trailed kisses to her ear. His hand roamed under the loose top and cupped her heavy breasts. He wanted to ravage her and seduce her, take her hard and cherish her gently.

She moaned, her hands gripping his shoulders. "Me too. I thought I'd missed my chance."

"What chance?" he asked absently. He released her breasts and fumbled with the buttons holding her pajama shirt together.

Her hands slid to the open front of his jeans again and her thumb brushed the damp head of his cock. "The chance to taste you."

He froze. Penta was a joyful and cooperative lover, but she'd never offered this before and he hadn't asked. "You don't have to."

"I want to." She lowered to her knees and shoved fabric out of her way. Her eyes gleamed up at him. "Penta Unleashed, remember?"

Her mouth closed over him, and he groaned. Her hands found his and brought them to her skull. He needed no more urging, gripping her firmly and holding her exactly where he wanted her, hips pulsing, encouraged by her moans as she sucked and licked.

Electric energy gathered at the base of his spine, tightening his balls. "Stop. Wait."

She ignored him, making delighted, approving noises as her mouth worked him.

"Penta. I'm going to—" He jerked uncontrollably, driving his cock deeper.

She drew her lips off slowly, her tongue teasing. "You don't want to finish this way?"

"Fuck, yeah, I do. But not tonight." He lifted her from the floor, and they tumbled onto the bed.

Penta licked her lips, savouring Cash's taste. He'd bucked into her mouth, his bullish grace shredded by her touch, and she'd loved wielding her power.

Now he hovered above her, braced on his palms, silver eyes molten like mercury. "You liked that, didn't you?"

She nodded vigorously and a gleam of amusement softened the intense creases around his eyes.

"Don't worry. We'll do it again. Soon."

She shivered with anticipation.

In moments they were both naked, though whose hands removed whose clothing was a jumbled confusion. Cash's mouth conquered her body, his hands teasing with sweet torture, until she squirmed in abandon.

"Now. Please." She panted and pleaded as he drove her to the edge but didn't let her slide over.

"Tell me." His fingers fluttered over her slick folds. "Tell me again."

"I love you." She clamped her thighs around his questing fingers. "I need you."

The growl that thundered from his chest was primitive and raw. Her legs fell open and he probed deeper. He stroked her core as he fed on her breast and her orgasm shattered, hurtling her into the cosmos of her mind.

She was still gasping from the force of it when he nestled between her knees and plunged inside. Delicate nerve-endings sparked into flame again and she clung to him, heels under his buttocks, hands on his back. Her whispered encouragements mingled with his hoarse, roaring breaths. His motions grew frantic, uncoordinated. With one last, deliciously punishing invasion, he stiffened, exploded, and collapsed on top of her.

Cash had never liked the term "making love." He'd thought it coy, needlessly discreet, and ill-suited for the messy, primitive, raucous delight of fucking.

He understood it now. Sex with someone you loved and who loved you back, with someone you knew to the depths of your soul and who knew you the same way?

Well, it was different. That's all he could say.

As he held a limp and satiated Penta and listened to her soft snores, he marveled at the difference a day made. There were still things they had to deal with—ignoring Tyrone wouldn't make him go away, for one—but he could face the morning knowing he was part of a team. That he wouldn't have to struggle alone. That someone had his back.

It was an odd feeling—and one he vowed never to take for granted.

He lay on his side, Penta's head heavy on his bicep, her ass snuggled perfectly against his groin. As much as he didn't want to disturb her, his shoulder was starting to ache. He shifted, easing out from under, and stretched out on his back.

She followed, her eyes fluttering open, the curve of her shoulder and hip silhouetted against the moonlit window. "Hey, there."

"Hey." A goofy grin curved his lips. Her answering smile looked as giddy as his felt and he wondered again at the miracle that was love.

"Why aren't you sleeping?" Her breasts pressed against his side and his cock stirred on his thigh.

"Not tired."

"You need to rest." Her fingertips feathered under his eyes.

"I don't want to miss anything."

Her drowsy expression softened further. "Don't worry. I'm not going anywhere." She snuggled in, draping a knee over his thigh and resting her hand on his chest. "And neither are you." Her fingers toyed with the hairs there for a few moments and then stilled as her breath evened out once more.

Her quiet declaration rang with fierce sincerity. He closed his eyes and let it lull him into a deep and peaceful slumber.

Chapter Thirty-Four

"Are you sure you want to do this?" Cash gripped Penta's hand, preventing her from entering Golden Dragon Tattoos. "I don't want you to regret it. Trust me. I have lots of ink I wish I hadn't gotten."

She could admit she was nervous, but about the potential pain, not the tattoo she'd chosen. "Are you going to regret getting this one?"

His answer was a kiss so forceful, so demanding, it drove all thoughts from her head. "I could never regret anything to do with you."

Dizzy and distracted, she had only one reply. "The same goes for me."

Helen greeted them with boisterous delight as they entered the studio. "I've set you up in the big room so you can be together while we do this. Cash, you'll be with Roberta. She's one of my new artists, but very good. Penta, you're with Jamie. They're my most experienced, and I thought you'd feel more comfortable knowing that."

As Helen and her team buzzed around getting everything settled, Penta tried to relax. The atmosphere reminded her of the dentist—the scent of antiseptic, the tray of unfamiliar instruments, the smoothly upholstered reclining chair.

Cash chatted with Jamie, who he seemed to remember from a previous visit years ago. His laughter rolled out, deep and rumbly, and she was struck by the change in him during the last couple of weeks. The grim gruff loner surfaced once in a while, but more and more she saw his generous joyful side.

Since the night he'd presented her with the Baby Bonnie, they'd spent all their non-working time together. At first, she'd wondered if he was worried Tyrone might try to wreak more havoc and didn't want to leave her alone just in case. About ten days ago, though, he'd mentioned he'd had a chat with his ex-friend and they'd sorted things out. She hadn't asked what the chat involved, but as Cash appeared to believe any danger was past, she was prepared to believe it too.

Jamie took a seat on a stool and rolled up next to Penta. "Ready?"

Taking a deep breath, she laid her right forearm knuckles down on the rest jutting from the chair and nodded. As Jamie poised the machine over her skin, Penta turned her head away and groped for Cash's hand. "Distract me."

Since Cash's arms were already covered in ink, he'd decided to get his tattoo on his right shoulder blade. He was facing the opposite direction from Penta, straddling a bench with his bare chest leaning against a hygienically paper-covered support. Propping his chin on the attached headrest, he took her hand in his left and smiled.

"Are you nervous about going back to school?"

She shot him a glare. "That's your solution? Distract me with the one thing that I'm even more terrified about?" A bee sting near her inner wrist made Penta twitch and she hissed in a breath.

"You're the bravest person I know. And I'm proud of you for taking this chance."

The email had arrived the day before. She'd been certain it would be a rejection and had opened it with calm acceptance. It had taken multiple reads of the contents before she'd believed the news. She'd had to put her head between her knees to recover from the shock.

"Things are going to get crazy." She kept her focus on Cash as the pricking transitioned to a scratching sensation. "I don't know how I'm going to balance everything."

"You'll figure it out."

His confidence eased the quivering in her gut. She squeezed his hand. "*We'll* figure it out. You're a part of this too."

"The kids will step up and help." His thumb rubbed the back of her hand. "You've raised them right. They'll be fine taking on more responsibility."

"I know." It wasn't just lip service. She did know. Her children were strong and resilient young men and women. It was time to show she trusted them by letting them make their own choices, their own mistakes.

While she kept a close eye on them, of course. She was still their mother, after all.

Cash shifted his feet without disturbing Roberta. "How do you think dinner with Hadiyyah went? I liked her."

Delilah and Abra had returned from Mexico two days ago, and Penta had held a welcome home party last night. At her urging, Felix had brought Hadiyyah to meet everyone.

"Me too." The short sharp scratches on her forearm were getting easier to ignore. "She's a lovely girl. Felix seems very smitten. He couldn't take his eyes off her."

"While I, on the other hand, couldn't take my eyes off you." He winked and her skin rippled in response. "And you, on the other *other* hand, couldn't take your eyes off the girls."

"I know they were only gone a month, but they seemed so grown up. Especially Abra. She's not a little girl anymore."

"They'll always be your girls."

"I know, but it's not the same. I'm glad they had a great time." And was even more glad that both had run toward her and clung to her with tears and laughter the moment they'd seen her. Maybe absence did make the heart grow fonder, even between mothers and daughters.

Penta's expression went soft and misty. Cash didn't think he'd ever grow tired of watching her emotions play over her face. She rarely hid what she was feeling, unashamed to show her heart to the world.

He could feel Roberta tracing lines on his shoulder blade, the discomfort familiar. On the other side of Penta's chair, Jamie made an adjustment to the machine and then returned to their work.

"What made you decide to get a tattoo?" It was a question he'd wanted to ask for several days, ever since Penta had told him her plan.

A blush swept up her neck and into her cheeks. "Well, I like yours."

"You do?" She'd never mentioned that before. The buzzing behind him changed pitch and Roberta shifted to a new place on his shoulder.

"Yeah. They're sexy." She bit her lip and slid him a shy glance. "I thought you might think the same of one on me."

"I do now." At first, he'd been dismayed at the idea of Penta marking her soft silky skin. But when she'd explained her idea for the design, he'd known he had to get the same one too.

It was simple but personal and as it was just lines and a clean font didn't take too long to complete. Still, his back was stiff by the time Roberta drew the final ink.

"There." She tapped Cash's elbow. "All done. Want a look?" She handed him a mirror and held another up at his back.

He studied the ink closely, pleased with the result. "Thanks, Roberta. It looks great."

Swinging his legs over the bench, he faced Penta.

Jamie turned off the other machine and the room fell silent. Helen popped her head in. "All done? How did it go?"

Penta moved her arm gingerly off the rest and studied it. "I love it," she said softly.

Near her inner wrist was a pentagram. Stretching toward her elbow was the word "unleashed." With a dollar sign instead of an S.

Cash had the ridiculous impulse to beat his chest like a caveman. Penta had marked herself with his symbol, with the nickname he had given her. It was her way of showing how committed she was to him. To them.

He cupped her chin in his hand and drew her gaze away from the design. "You're mine. Now and forever." Ignoring the very interested audience, he kissed her long and deep. When he pulled back, she was delightfully dazed, her lips swollen and pink.

"And you're mine." She urged him to twist so she could see his back. Her lips brushed his red and sensitive flesh. "Today and always."

THANKS FOR READING
Too Good for Words.

Reviews and ratings are a great way to help other readers discover new authors. Just a line or two is all that's needed—or simply click the number of stars you think it deserves. I encourage you to post your honest opinion at the retailer where you purchased your copy, on GoodReads and BookBub. Thank you so much!

Visit my website to discover more titles in the Silverberry Seduction Seasoned Romance Series.

I'd love to stay in touch. Subscribe to my newsletter and you'll immediately receive Margin of Risk, a companion short story in the Silverberry Seduction world. You'll also be able to tag along with my dog-walking adventures, find out what I'm reading when I should be working, and other randomness...along with all my writing news, of course! Find the sign-up form at www.brendamargriet.com.

PENTA'S CHOCOLATE CHIP COOKIE RECIPE

1 cup margarine, softened, cut into chunks
1 cup white sugar
1 cup brown sugar

1 teaspoon vanilla
2 eggs, beaten
2 1/3 cup flour
1 teaspoon baking soda
½ teaspoon salt

1 cup chocolate chips

Using hand blender, mix first three ingredients well.
Add vanilla and eggs and blend.
Add next five ingredients and mix well.
Add chocolate chips and mix well.

Drop onto cookie sheet and bake in 375F oven for 8 to 10 minutes.

ABOUT THE AUTHOR

Brenda Margriet writes savvy, slow burn, contemporary romances with ordinarily amazing characters. In her own ordinarily amazing life, she had a successful career in radio and television production before deciding to pilfer from her retirement plan to support her writing compulsion.

Readers have called her stories "poignant," "explicit and steamy," "interesting, intriguing and entertaining," and "unlike any romance you've read before" (she assumes the latter was meant in a good way).

Join Brenda on social media—she is most active on Facebook and Instagram. And you can always discover more about her and her books on her website, brendamargriet.com.

ALSO BY BRENDA MARGRIET

SILVERBERRY SEDUCTION SEASONED
ROMANCE
Secrets Under the Covers
Loving Between the Lines
Turn the Next Page
Strictly by the Book
Too Good for Words
The Complete Silverberry Seduction Series
(e-book only)

TIMELESS SEASONED ROMANCE
After Words
Richly Deserved

THE BENDIXON SISTERS SERIES
Allegro Court
Gateway Crescent
Crossroads Corner
Taking His Measure: The Complete Bendixon
Sisters Series (e-book only)

STANDALONE READS
Mountain Fire
Reserved for You
No Life But This
When Time Falls Still
The Promise of Frost

Read excerpts and find buy links at
www.brendamargriet.com

www.ingramcontent.com/pod-product-compliance
Lightning Source LLC
Chambersburg PA
CBHW030820020726
47499CB00006B/2006